MISTLETOE BACHELORS

Jennifer Snow

Mainstream Romance

Secret Cravings Publishing
www.secretcravingspublishing.com

A Secret Cravings Publishing Book
Mainstream Romance

Mistletoe Bachelors
Copyright © 2012 Jennifer Snow
Print ISBN: 978-1-61885-666-1

First E-book Publication: November 2012
First Print Publication: April 2013

Cover design by Dawne Dominique
Edited by Mary Clark
Proofread by Marja Salmon
All cover art and logo copyright © 2012 by Secret Cravings
Publishing

PUBLISHER
Secret Cravings Publishing
www.secretcravingspublishing.com

Dedication
For my Grandmother Hanlon. Thank you for your
continued love and support.

MISTLETOE BACHELORS

Jennifer Snow

Copyright © 2012

Chapter One

This submission was the worst one yet. Madison Grey glanced at the man awaiting her response to his article proposal. "Thank you for your submission, but it's not *quite* what we had in mind." Behind her forced smile, her brain was frantic. In two months, not one decent Christmas themed article had crossed her desk. Time was running out, but she refused to publish a story about Santa's forgotten elf in a women's quarterly magazine. She slid the problem-filled manuscript toward its owner. This new face-to-face submission process was draining. *What was her boss thinking to implement such a crazy policy*?

Cole Harris smiled.

Madison sighed. *That won't work.* She didn't doubt those handsome upturned lips often did the trick, but not with her. Tall, dark, and handsome with a fantastic smile used to be her type. Now she preferred her men at a distance. She knew the type, and she was about as far from interested in him romantically, as she was in his disappointing submission.

She turned in her chair and straightened her pencil skirt as she stood, "A pleasure meeting you. Good luck with the writing." She extended a hand to Cole.

He took it in his, and his grip tightened around her slender hand. "So you won't publish the story?" Cole remained seated. His eyes left hers to travel the length of her thin frame. They paused on her long bare legs.

Her eyes narrowed. *Seriously?* She tugged her hand away and supressed the urge to sigh. *Why were they always so hard to get rid of?* She took a deep breath searching for the most professional way to tell him the article was awful. "As I've explained Mr. Harris, the magazine is featuring Christmas romance stories next month, and your article would be better suited for...well, children." *Or the garbage can under my desk.* She walked toward her office door aware of the piercing blue eyes watching her every step. Uncomfortable under his gaze, she opened the door and hid behind it.

Cole stood and joined her. He rolled the typewritten pages and tucked them into the inside pocket of his leather jacket.

"I have another meeting shortly, so if you'll excuse me..." Madison glanced at her watch and gestured for him to leave. She'd had about as much as she could take this week with the number of awful submissions she'd rejected, the part of the job she enjoyed least. However, Cole didn't look as disappointed as the other rejects.

An amused smile spread across his face. "How about I take you to lunch, and maybe you could give me some pointers? You know...help me with the writing." He slid into his leather jacket and checked his watch.

"That's not part of my job." Madison stiffened. *Was he seriously hitting on her?* She fought to hide her annoyance. "Ashley, our receptionist can provide you with a list of critique groups if you're interested." *Please go away.* He'd wasted enough of her time already.

"How about just lunch then? You do eat?" Once again his eyes took in her tall, slender figure.

Not lately. A lunch break was a luxury these days as her workload increased with the holiday season, and the December issue deadline was drawing near. Every morning, her coffee went cold before she could finish it, and it was well after dark before she left the office most evenings. She tucked a stray lock of long brown hair behind her ear and folded her arms across her chest. "I can't."

"Fine, dinner tonight. That's my final offer." Cole leaned against the doorframe.

Madison's eyes narrowed "No." *This guy was persistent.* "Ashley's desk is the last one on the right." She pointed down the hall. "She will be happy to help you." *In more ways than one I'm sure.*

"Okay, I'm leaving." Cole held his hands up in defeat and shook his head as he walked past her out into the hall. "Enjoy the rest of your day. I'll see you around." He gave a quick wave as he headed down the hall toward the elevators.

God, I hope not. She stood in the otherwise empty hallway staring after him. *Where had she seen him before?* The nagging feeling, she knew him from somewhere, had plagued her from the moment he'd entered her office.

"Wasn't that, Cole Harris?" Her friend and co-worker, Samantha, poked her head out of the copy room across the hall.

"Yes. *Please* tell me where I recognize him from." *So, he was someone she should know.*

"Madison, that was, *Cole Harris*." Samantha shot her a look of disbelief. She added more paper to the photocopier and shut the tray.

"Yes, that part, I know." Madison gestured for Samantha to continue.

Samantha stood and rolled her eyes. "Cole Harris, the most popular journalistic photographer in New York. His photos appear in the New York Times almost daily." Adoration was evident in her voice. "And what a cutie." Samantha leaned down the hall, watching Cole disappear inside the elevator.

"I hadn't noticed." Madison went back into her office and opened her *Outlook* calendar. *Meeting with her boss in twenty minutes.* The reminder was unnecessary. *How could she forget about a meeting she'd been anxiously anticipating for a week?*

Samantha joined her in the office and took a seat across from her. "Yeah, right. You might have sworn off men, but you're not blind. What was he doing in your office?"

"Who?" Madison looked puzzled.

Samantha rolled her eyes. "Cole Harris!"

Oh, right. "He submitted a manuscript." Madison typed, *Cole Harris* into *Google* search. *Aha. That's where she'd seen him before.* The New York Times had presented him with a photography award, three years before at a journalism banquet in Manhattan. The same year, Madison had been awarded editor of the year. A lifetime ago it seemed. The memory crossed her mind of what had been one the best and worse nights of her life. Her husband had missed the award dinner, one of the greatest moments in her career, claiming he was working late at the law firm. She shivered at the memory of arriving at his office, award in hand to discover him working on undressing his legal assistant. A month later, she'd moved to Staten Island, three weeks before Christmas. This time of year made her crazy. She studied the picture of the handsome photographer. He couldn't be much older than her twenty-eight years.

"Weird. I didn't know he could write too." Samantha peered over Madison's shoulder, surveying the pictures on the screen.

"He can't." Madison shut the search engine and turned her attention to her friend. Big snowflake earrings hung from Samantha's ears. "Where do you buy the crazy Christmas jewelry?"

"What's wrong with my jewelry?" Samantha pretended to pout. "You know, it wouldn't hurt you to be a little more festive." She scanned Madison's office, the only one in the building not decorated for the season.

"You know, I don't do Christmas." Madison frowned at the thought. At one time, Christmas had been her favorite time of year. She'd cherished the familiar holiday traditions—the hustle and bustle of last minute Christmas shopping, the tree lighting ceremony in the park and curling up in front of a fireplace on Christmas Eve. Since the divorce, she'd found more than enough excuses to avoid the festivities.

Samantha sighed, looking around the office, void of personal touches. "I know, I just think it wouldn't hurt to have a small tree or something…"

"Drop it. We've had this discussion. I'm not putting a tree in here or anything else with a fake pine smell." Madison wrinkled her nose and pointed a finger at her friend. "And don't even think about spraying my windows with that, snow from a can crap, like you did last year."

"Fine. Be a Grinch." Samantha lowered her voice, as she closed Madison's office door and took the seat Cole Harris had just vacated. "Hey, guess what I heard?"

"That the new owners are planning to make some big changes to the magazine next year?" Madison took a sip of her cold coffee and grimaced. The company had been sold earlier that year, and so far things had remained the same. She suspected that wouldn't be the case for long.

Samantha nodded. "I feel a promotion coming for you." She swivelled in the office chair and smiled.

"I don't know about a promotion, but more work looms on the horizon." *Of that she was sure.* Her boss had told her a week before—he had a new assignment for her. It required traveling throughout most of the holiday season. She'd jumped at the opportunity to avoid Christmas, at least in the traditional sense. It *had* to be a writing assignment. Her long awaited opportunity to prove she could write for the magazine.

"Kim in circulation told Marge in marketing that they are also starting to bring in freelance writers and photographers to help with the advertising campaigns for the New Year." Her friend interrupted her thoughts.

"Freelance writers?" A frown clouded Madison's soft features.

"Oh, but I wouldn't worry…" Samantha shook her head. "I'm sure the main articles will still be assigned to staff writers."

Madison wasn't convinced. *Freelance writers.* She didn't like the idea.

"So, when is your meeting with Damian?"

"This afternoon." Madison glanced at her watch. "In twelve minutes actually…Sorry, I guess lunch is out of the question. You know how Damian is about being on time." Their boss was a clock-watcher.

"Don't worry, go. I can't wait to hear about it. I'll keep my fingers crossed for you." Samantha stood and opened the office door.

"Thanks." Madison drained the cold contents of her coffee cup. She had a feeling she would need it.

* * * *

Eleven minutes later, Madison stopped cold, as she saw Cole Harris waiting near the office elevator. *What was he still doing here? Man, the guy obviously couldn't take* no *for an answer.* Dealing with him would make her late for the meeting. She bit her lip and hesitated. Maybe she should take the stairs.

He turned, and his eyes met hers. He grinned.

Shit, he saw her. She couldn't run away from him now. "If you're here to ask me out again…" Madison joined him next to the elevator, annoyance creeping into her voice.

He held his hands up in defense. "I'm not."

"You're not?" She folded her arms across her chest, and eyed him with suspicion. She glanced at her watch. *Forty-two seconds. She'd have to sprint from the elevator.* She looked down at her four-inch stilettos. *Maybe Damian's clock would be slow.*

"I have another meeting," Cole said, as the elevator doors opened.

Madison rushed inside. "Mr. Harris, if you're planning to meet with another editor to try to get that story published, it won't do you any good. Here, at *Women's World,* we all adhere to the same policies and guidelines. Your story doesn't fit. You won't get your work published here." *There she said it. How much clearer could she be without sounding rude?* The elevator numbers lit up one by one. Four, five, six…

Cole grinned and leaned against the wall, studying her. "Are you sure about that?"

"Absolutely."   Twenty-six   seconds.   Nine,   ten, eleven…*Damian's clock better not be fast.* She shifted her weight from one foot to the other.

"We'll see." He winked.

The elevator doors opened on the fourteenth floor.

She dashed into the hall.

He followed.

"Fine, whatever." In less than nine seconds she was ready to argue her case about why she deserved a writing assignment, if Damian wasn't offering one. The last thing she needed to concern herself with was Cole Harris. She'd let another editor deal with him. She rounded the corner at the end of the hall.

Cole did the same.

She glanced back at him. *Where is he going?* Damian's office was the only office down this hallway. *Oh no.* She turned and collided with his solid chest. He was bigger and taller than he'd appeared earlier in her office. Up close, his light blue eyes were almost gray. She shook her head. *Who cares what color his eyes are?*

"Where do you think you're going?" She glared. Her watch beeped indicating the hour. *So close.* She sighed.

"You're really intense for such a tiny person." He grabbed her shoulders to steady her.

"You have a meeting with Damian? Now?" She yanked free from his grasp. *What was going on?* Damian hadn't mentioned anyone else would be attending the meeting.

"Yes, and you made us late." Cole grinned, as he opened Damian's office door and shoved her inside.

She stumbled on the plush, tan carpet and her eyes narrowed as her gaze met Cole's.

"Good, you two have already met." Damian greeted as they entered. "Come on in, grab a seat. We have a lot to discuss."

"Damian, pleasure to see you again." Cole extended a hand and smiled at the older man behind the mahogany desk.

Madison watched the exchange, more uncomfortable by the second. *What had she signed on for this holiday season?*

* * * *

Cole hit the button on the pole at the crosswalk for a walk signal and paced back and forth on the crowded sidewalk to keep warm. A light snow fell and melted as it hit the ground, creating dirty slush puddles on the street. The sky was overcast and dark and the crisp air pierced through his clothing, but even the unfavorable weather couldn't destroy his good mood.

The light turned to walk, and he hummed as he crossed the busy street. He couldn't believe his luck. This Christmas season had gotten considerably more appealing. *Women's World Quarterly* was one of the fastest growing women's magazines in the state, and a six-page photo spread in its holiday edition would do wonders for his career. The two-week long travel assignment to document the holiday traditions of some of New York's finest men would be a great kick-start to the season. Of course, taking pictures of five dudes while they celebrated the holidays wasn't top on his list of things to photograph, but at least, he knew two of them. Bachelor number one, Scott Thompson and number three Blake Ford had only agreed to the assignment because of his persuasion. He grinned. Having the editor-in-chief of *Women's World Quarterly* owe him a favor was a great position to be in. Add a generous expense account and a sexy as hell travel companion, and this would be a great trip.

He paused at the next set of lights and shoved his hands in his pockets. The corner of a business card poked his finger and he pulled it out as he crossed the street. *Madison Grey, Senior Editor.* The woman was exactly as everyone had warned. Tough, stubborn and determined. And incredibly beautiful. He'd met her before, briefly, at the New York Times award dinner three years before. At the time, she'd been married to some lawyer in Manhattan. Rumor had it, the guy had a wandering eye and the marriage lasted less than three years. Cole shook his head. *How anyone could stray from Madison Grey's sexy legs, he'd never understand.*

He chuckled at the memory of her pretty features, as she'd read his submission. The story, written by his young niece for an elementary school homework assignment, had been meant as a joke. However, when she'd taken it seriously, he'd played along. He wanted to meet her before their meeting with Damian, but it had soon become clear, she had no idea who he was or about the assignment she was being given. An assignment, he suspected she wasn't thrilled about. She'd remained silent throughout the meeting and her face had paled when the bachelor list was presented. Her reaction surprised him. Most women he knew would have jumped at the opportunity to interview these handsome, successful men. He wondered why Madison was the exception.

Cole pushed open the door to the *Starbucks* on the corner. The smell of fresh-brewed coffee and cinnamon spiced scones made his stomach growl. He loosened his borrowed tie and unbuttoned his shirt as he waited in line. He hated wearing a tie. He didn't know how those corporate guys, like his brother-in-law, wore one every day.

His cell phone rang, and he reached into his pocket. *Women's World Quarterly* flashed on the display screen. *She missed him already?* He grinned and cocked his head to the side as he accepted the call. "Hello?"

"Cole Harris?"

The voice was not Madison's.

"That's me." He covered the receiver as he reached the counter. A pretty, petite redhead waited to take his order.

Her smile was coy, as she twirled a piece of hair around her finger. "What can I get started for you?"

"A gingerbread latte please." He said with a wink, reaching into his back pocket for his wallet.

The young barista blushed and dashed off to make the latte.

Cole turned his attention back to the call.

"Mr. Harris, this is Ashley from *Women's World*. We have your travel itinerary confirmed. We can email you a copy if that's more convenient," she paused before adding, "or you could stop by…"

Cole smiled. The young receptionist had flirted with him twice that day. She was cute. Maybe he'd bring her a latte. Maybe convince her to help him with something—like Madison's address.

He gestured to the barista. "Make that two…to go." Then into the phone, "I'll stop by to pick it up."

"Great." The girl purred. "See you soon, Mr. Harris."

Cole disconnected the call and paid for the lattes, tossing the change into the tip jar on the counter. "Thanks." He waved as he left the store.

The girl smiled and tossed her red curls over her shoulder as she turned her attention to the next customer in line.

Outside, Cole shivered and brought one of the steaming cups to his lips. Red lipstick on the side caught his attention. "Britney-475-5693". He grinned. *If only they were all that easy.*

Chapter Two

"Madison, that's your fourth cosmopolitan in an hour, you may want to—never mind." Samantha said, as a waiter arrived with two more drinks for Madison.

Mulhalley's Pub, the popular after work grill and pub had become their favorite Friday night girls spot. Tonight was Tuesday, and Madison never drank during the week.

Madison drained the contents of the glass in her hand and reached for another.

Samantha moved it out of reach. "Just start from the beginning, and tell me what happened. It can't be that bad."

Madison refused to talk about her new assignment all afternoon, locking herself in her office under a pile of work. She'd emailed Samantha to meet her at *Mulhalley's* after work, skipping their usual Tuesday night yoga class.

"Come on, Madison. Did you not receive the writing assignment?" A worried expression crossed Samantha's face. She leaned forward, across the table in the booth, to be heard above the noise in the pub.

Loud Christmas music played from a speaker above their heads. *Jeez, Christmas music already?* It was only the first of December. The festivities seemed to start earlier every year. Madison frowned. "Oh, I got the assignment." She nodded.

"That's great—isn't it?" Confusion spread across Samantha's petite features. "This *is* what you wanted, right?"

Madison nodded, and then shook her head. Her shoulders sagged as she took another sip of her cosmopolitan. She wanted a writing assignment, just not *this* one.

"Yes? No? I'm confused. Madison what's wrong?" Exasperation filled Samantha's voice.

She couldn't leave her friend in suspense any longer. She took a deep breath. "Cole Harris for one thing." She slumped forward in her seat. "He's so arrogant, and he thinks that sexy smile of his can get him anything he wants."

"Besides the obvious fact that it can. What does Cole Harris's smile have to do with your assignment?" Samantha picked up her wine glass and took a sip.

"It's a travel assignment interviewing five of New York's finest bachelors on their holiday traditions..." She explained, rolling her eyes. As if women cared about how five of the most arrogant, unattainable men in New York would be spending their holidays. *Okay, maybe some women cared.* She *didn't.*

"So, you have to interview him." Samantha shrugged. "Twenty minutes alone with him won't kill you. In fact, I'd spend twenty minutes alone with him any day."

Madison shot her an annoyed look.

"What? He's hot."

Madison shook her head. "Anyway, that's not it. He's traveling with me to photograph the bachelors."

"Madison, forgive me for saying this, but there are far worse fates in life than to have to travel with a gorgeous, successful man during one of the most romantic times of year. You're overreacting." Samantha sat back in her chair and relaxed.

"You haven't heard the worst part yet." Madison rested her head on her arm on the table.

Samantha reached across and picked up her forehead, forcing her friend to look at her. "Well, what is it? And if you say you have an unlimited expense account, I'm out of here."

"Kurt." Madison dropped her head back against the table with a thud.

"Your ex-husband? What does he have to do with—oh no!" Samantha clasped a hand over her mouth.

Madison nodded in confirmation.

"You have to interview him?"

Madison nodded again.

"Oh, Madison." Samantha pushed the drinks in Madison's direction as she listened.

"I know—ironic, isn't it? I finally land the assignment I've been asking for, and it turns out to be the assignment from hell. I don't enjoy the Christmas season or spending time in Manhattan, and I'm definitely not excited about seeing Kurt again." She shuddered. Even the sound of her ex-husband's name made her cringe.

"Why did you accept the assignment?" Samantha looked at her with concern.

"How could I refuse? I have begged Damian for a writing assignment for months." She shook her head. "I had to accept. Besides, it wasn't as if I had a choice. You should have seen the two of them." Madison's tone grew angry. "They planned the entire itinerary without once consulting me." It wasn't the exact truth. They had asked her input, but she'd been too stunned by the whole thing to do more than nod in agreement.

"When do you start?" Samantha flagged the waiter for their bill.

"We, Cole and I, leave first thing tomorrow morning on the seven o'clock ferry to Manhattan." Madison looked distressed, holding her head in her hands. On such short notice, she hadn't even had time to process the whole thing yet.

"Seven o'clock ferry? Ouch, that's early." Samantha said, looking at the empty glasses in front of her friend.

Madison followed her gaze. She wasn't a morning person, add a hangover, and she would feel awful. *Why had she drank so much?* This wasn't her usual way of dealing with her stress. She should have gone to their usual yoga class. Though she suspected no amount of deep breathing would help ease the tension seeping through her neck and shoulders.

"Let's get you some coffee and get you home. I have a feeling tomorrow morning will be here faster than you're going to like."

* * * *

The sound of *Jingle Bell Rock* filled Madison's room early the next morning.

She opened one sleepy eye and peered at the alarm clock on the bedside table. "Five thirty? Are you kidding me?" She groaned, burying her head under the pillow. *Why hadn't she insisted on a later ferry to Manhattan?* They weren't interviewing the first bachelor until the following day. She frowned. Of course, Cole Harris had suggested the extra day for preparation. She remembered he'd mentioned something about picking up supplies from his studio in the city. "Hmph." She fumbled with the alarm clock until she found the *off* button and slammed it twice.

The smell of coffee filled her room. *Coffee? Had she set the maker last night?* She sat up straight, pushing the pillow aside. *Samantha.* She smiled. *Thank God for her friend.* Madison yawned as she made her way to the bathroom. She smiled when she saw her favorite red sweater and charcoal dress pants lying over her chaise in the corner of the room. *What would she do without her friend?* She climbed into the shower, and as the hot water trickled down her back, she forced herself to think of the next three weeks as a stepping stone in her career and not an experience that might kill her. Her long awaited opportunity to prove herself in the world of journalism. Sure, it was just for the holiday edition, but she was confident once Damian saw her potential, writing assignments would be a regular thing. With the new changes occurring in the New Year, she hoped to move away from the editing department for good.

As she finished flat ironing her long dark hair, the doorbell rang. *Her landlord coming to collect her rent check?* Grabbing her purse, she opened the door.

Cole Harris stood on the other side.

Her mouth fell open as her gaze met his. "What are you doing here?" Annoyance filled her voice.

"I thought we could drive to the ferry together." He smiled. "And good morning to you too." He handed her a cup of coffee.

"How did you get in here?" Madison scanned the hallways. This was a secure building. Someone must have broken the rule set by the strata committee against allowing unregistered guests into the building.

"Moving guys outside let me in. I helped them carry a couch." Cole said with a shrug.

Madison shook her head. "That's fantastic." She took a deep breath and cleared her throat. "Anyway, I was planning to take a taxi…" She explained, accepting the coffee cup with reluctance. It smelled too wonderful to resist, even if it would be cup number four so far that morning.

"Now you don't have to." Cole said. "Are you ready to go or can I come in?" He tucked a hand into his jeans pocket.

"I'll just be a minute." Madison stepped back to let him in. "Wait a second, how did you get my address?" She blocked the entrance to her apartment.

"I stopped by reception at the magazine office yesterday afternoon, and they gave it to me." He sipped his own coffee and peered at her over the rim.

"What? We have a policy against giving out personal private information. Who did you talk to?" She could guess.

"Alisha? Petite blonde at reception." He shrugged.

Figures. Ashley. She didn't bother to correct him. "That explains it." No doubt his charm hadn't gone unnoticed or unappreciated by the young blonde receptionist. "I'm sure she sang like a canary the moment you flashed that sexy..." She stopped and turned away, grabbing her jacket from the hook behind the door.

Cole grinned and cocked his head to the side. "You think I have a sexy something? What is it?" He reached to help her with her coat.

She moved away. "Nothing." She pushed him through the open door and closed it behind them.

"I bet it's my butt." He grinned, leaning against the wall in the hallway.

She locked her apartment door.

"Am I right? I saw you checking me out in your office yesterday." He took a sip of his coffee.

"I definitely was not." Madison let out a deep breath. "I just meant, some people might give in to your charm, that's all." She struggled with the large suitcase, dragging it down the hall.

He took it from her. "But, not you?"

"Not me." She shook her head.

"Are you sure?" He paused.

"Without a doubt." She snatched back the handle of the suitcase and continued down the hall.

His laughter followed her. "This is going to be fun."

She didn't dare question what he meant.

* * * *

Madison closed her eyes and sunk deeper into the bubbles in her whirlpool tub in her hotel room later that evening. *Ahhh.* The scent of Jasmine invigorated her senses, and the tension in her shoulders melted away. The late night and early morning had been a bad combination, and she planned to be in bed by eight o'clock. Her cell phone rang in the other room. The generic ringtone, not one of the person-specific ones she'd applied. She ignored it. *Whoever it was, could leave a message.* She reached outside of the tub and picked up her novel. She flipped the pages with sudsy hands and readjusted her back against the plastic, water cushion.

The hotel room phone rang. *Who was that?* Few people knew where she was. Dropping the book, she stood and reached for a towel.

The phone rang a third time.

"I'm coming," she grumbled, sliding her feet into the terry cloth slippers.

She picked up the receiver on the fourth ring. "Hello?"

Dial tone.

"Argh." She glared at the phone and slammed it back in place.

A loud knock rapped on her door, and she jumped. "Who is it?"

"Room service," was the reply.

Must have the wrong room. Though room service did sound like a good idea. Maybe this guy could take her order. She swung the door open. "I didn't order…" She stopped.

Cole stood in the hallway.

When was the last time she'd opened a door, and he wasn't standing there?

The smell of Chinese food filled the hallway, and she didn't have to ask what he carried in the brown paper bag. A small artificial decorated Christmas tree sat propped against the doorframe.

"What is that?" Madison hid herself behind the door.

"Dinner." He wiggled the bag.

"I meant that." She pointed to the tree, not letting him inside. *What was he doing here anyway?* She hadn't agreed to have dinner with him. Attractive men were full of assumptions.

"A Christmas tree. I stole it from the lobby. I thought you might want to make your room a bit festive." He waited. "So, can I come in?"

Madison hesitated. She glanced at her towel. *Send him away.* Her stomach growled. "Yes to the food—and you, I guess, but, no to the tree. Leave it in the hall." Madison opened the door to let him in.

Cole ignored her and carried the tree inside. He placed it in the corner of the suite before setting the food on the desk, next to her open laptop.

Madison continued to shield herself with the hotel room door. "Close your eyes while I go to the bathroom."

"You know I have seen a woman in a towel before." Cole gave her an amused look as he opened the bag of food.

"I'm serious. Either close your eyes or leave." His scrutinizing gaze made her uneasy. Wearing a towel with her wet hair dripping down her back, she may as well be naked.

"How about I keep my back turned and unpack the food?" He continued removing the cardboard boxes from the bag.

"Fine. But *do not* turn around."

"You got it." Cole laughed.

Madison shut the door and grabbed a pair of jeans and sweater from her open suitcase. She dashed into the bathroom.

She re-entered a moment later.

Cole sat at the desk. "You writing a book or something?" His eyes were on her laptop screen.

She sighed. She'd meant to close the open document. "Don't read that." She flicked the laptop lid closed. Her cheeks flushed as she wondered how much he had read. "Haven't you ever heard of privacy?"

"It was open." He shrugged. "It was good." He smiled. "I especially liked the part about the guy's bulging biceps."

He was making fun of her. *Worse, her writing.* "Should we eat?" The faster they got through dinner, the faster she could resume her quiet evening of writing.

He handed her a box of beef and broccoli. "So, you're not a fan of the city, and you're a Grinch. Have I got it right so far?" Cole looked out the window overlooking the city with a cardboard box of rice in one hand and chopsticks in the other.

Madison sat cross-legged on her bed. "What makes you think I dislike the city?" Madison took a bite from her fork. Chopsticks were a waste of time. She was starving.

"When you fell asleep on the ferry, you kept mumbling about how you hate the city." He popped a chicken ball into his mouth.

Madison's eyes narrowed. "I don't talk in my sleep."

Cole nodded. "How would you know? You're asleep."

How would *she know?* It had been three years since she'd shared a bed with a man. She shook her head and let out a deep breath. "Fine, maybe I do."

"So, why?" Cole paused, chopsticks poised in mid-air. He looked at her expectantly.

"Why what?"

Cole rolled his eyes. "Why do you hate Manhattan?"

Madison shrugged. "I just prefer the quiet pace of Staten Island." The city life used to appeal to her. The hustle and bustle, the crowds, the noise—they were all part of the city's charm, but now she liked her peaceful, work-filled life on the Island.

"Okay, I'll buy that. So what's with the hate on you have for Christmas? Didn't get what you wanted from Santa last year?" He handed her a box of rice and took the beef and broccoli.

She studied the contents in the cardboard box, refusing to meet his gaze. Discussing the many reasons why the season made her depressed was off limits. She took a mouthful of rice and avoided his intense, curious gaze.

"I mean, I've seen your office. Not a Christmas decoration or holiday card...unlike the rest of the office, which looks like a group of elves on Prozac broke in and let loose." He laughed.

That elf would be Samantha. Madison sighed. "Christmas is...fine. I'm just way too busy to worry about decorating my office."

"I see." Cole drummed his fingers on the table. "Then why didn't you want to take this assignment if you wouldn't be celebrating Christmas anyway?"

Madison cringed. This guy had a gift for getting under her skin. "What makes you think I didn't want this assignment?" Had her feelings been that obvious? She hoped Damian hadn't noticed. She bit her lip.

"You went pale when Damian presented the bachelor line-up." Cole set the beef and broccoli aside.

He was too observant for her liking. If he wanted her to like him, he wasn't helping his cause. "I did not."

"You did." He nodded. "And you kept toying with that pendant you wear around your neck. A nervous habit of yours?" He stood and looked out the window overlooking the street.

She glared at his back and touched the script *M* on the white gold chain hanging around her neck. "So, I have an annoying habit. You're reading too much into it." Appetite gone, she folded the lid on the cardboard box.

"So, you're excited about the assignment?" His tone suggested he didn't believe her.

She didn't care. She didn't owe him an explanation about why this was the worse assignment she could have been given. She didn't even know him, and she planned to keep it that way. "Yes."

"But not about traveling with me?"

Damn, he was insightful. "Look, I'm sure you're delightful," *and sexy as hell*, "but I like my alone time, my down time at the end of the day." Away from these unwanted advances of a handsome heartbreaker.

"And you think I'm going to interfere?"

Madison cocked her head to the side. "You're in my hotel room uninvited." *Did he need reminding? He'd barged in here, disturbing her relaxing bath and plans to work on her manuscript.*

Cole stood and grabbed two fortune cookies from the desk. He tossed one to her and headed for the door.

She caught the cookie in one hand. "Where are you going?" She bit her lip and closed her eyes. *Who cares, he's leaving.*

"I'm leaving you alone. For now. But I'm warning you—I'm a cool guy. By the end of this trip you're going to want to spend time with me and I may not let you." He smiled and opened the door.

"I doubt it." Madison joined him at the door, her hands on her hips.

Cole chuckled. "Don't forget to water the tree," he called as he unlocked his room door and disappeared inside.

* * * *

Madison shifted in the passenger seat of Cole's truck, admiring the beautiful homes in the suburban neighborhood, twenty minutes from the city. The properties in this part of Manhattan ranged in the multi-million dollar range and housed some of New York's finest. Scott Thompson, bachelor number one was no exception. A commercial real estate broker, the forty-two year old enjoyed a lucrative lifestyle.

Cole pulled into the long circular driveway, and Madison gasped at the manicured garden veiled in snow. The three-story house had arching peaks at both ends of the rooftop and was painted a deep burgundy color, with dark wood accents and trim. A dream home in a picturesque winter setting with enormous Oak trees, which had long ago lost their leaves and now wore a draping of snow and ice, lined edges of the property. A family of snowmen, in full costume of hats, scarves and mittens decorated the lawn.

Cute family. Madison liked Scott Thompson already. *A hardworking father, who still made time for his two daughters*. She jotted a few notes in her notebook.

Cole shut off the truck and turned to face her. "I'll set up out here and take some exterior shots first, I'll meet you inside." He jumped from the truck and tossed his camera bag over one shoulder.

Madison nodded. She gathered her purse and notebook and climbed out of the truck.

"Madison Grey? Come on in." Scott opened the front door as she approached. He waved to Cole. "Just let yourself in when you're done."

"Hello." Madison smiled. Scott didn't look a day over thirty, with his sandy blond hair and hazel eyes. He was taller than she'd expected. Six foot two inches, she would guess. "Mr. Thompson, a pleasure to meet you. Thank you for inviting us into your home." She extended a hand.

"Please call me, Scott." He led the way into the living room.

"You have a fantastic home, Scott." Madison admired the spiral staircase leading to the upper levels of the home.

"It's a bit extravagant for me. My wife picked it out. She loved the staircase and the open foyer and the big yard for the girls." Scott's gaze landed on a photo of a beautiful woman in a flowing blue sundress sitting on a swing in their yard.

"She was beautiful." Madison smiled at the picture. Melissa Thompson had passed away two years before, after a six-year battle with cancer.

"She was incredible. You know, you think over time, it would get easier, but this time of year…" Scott gave a sad smile.

"I can't imagine how hard a loss like that must be." Madison surveyed the other framed family photos on the fireplace.

"I'd be lost without the girls. Here they come."

The sound of giggling filled the foyer as the two young girls raced into the living room.

Emma and Amelia Thompson looked like him but had their mother's dark hair and blue eyes. The combination was striking.

"Girls, come meet Madison. She's going to be hanging out with us for a few days." Scott waved them over to join him on the couch.

"Are you the new nanny?" the youngest, Emma asked from her hiding spot behind her father's leg.

"No she's writing a story about us, aren't you?" Amelia said.

"Yes, I am. If that's okay with you girls?" Madison sat in an armchair across from the girls.

Amelia nodded. "Sure. Emma likes to have her picture taken."

"So do you." The other little girl pouted, folding her arms across her tiny frame.

Madison laughed. "Cole is outside taking pictures, but he will be in soon."

Cole entered the living room. He rubbed his red hands together for warmth.

"Uncle Cole!" Emma ran and jumped into Cole's arms.

He caught her and spun her around the living room. The action was so natural. Madison swallowed a lump in her throat. An unexpected reaction to the sight.

"You're their uncle?" *He hadn't mentioned he knew any of the bachelors.* She shot him a quizzical look.

He nodded and shrugged, tickling Emma.

The little girl squealed in delight.

"Cole is Melissa's brother, my brother-in-law." Scott shook Cole's hand and slapped him on the back. "He's the only reason we agreed to do this. Good to see you."

Madison watched the familiar exchange between the two, and her eyes drifted back to the photograph of Melissa. The two could be twins.

Scott took Emma from him and set her back on the floor.

"Dad, now that Uncle Cole is here, can we eat the cookies we baked?" Amelia tugged on her father's shirt.

"It's only nine o'clock in the morning. Isn't that too early for cookies?" Scott smiled at his daughter.

Amelia looked disappointment.

"It's never too early for a cookie." Cole winked at Scott. He turned to Madison. "You eat cookies for breakfast all the time don't you?"

Amelia's eyes were hopeful as she looked between the adults.

"All the time." Madison nodded and smiled.

Scott shrugged and shook his head. "Okay then. I guess I've been outvoted. Let's go into the kitchen." He led the way.

Emma trailed behind and slid her hand into Madison's. She gestured for her to come closer.

Madison bent lower. "Yeah?"

"I've already eaten three." The little girl giggled.

* * * *

Madison's arms ached under the weight of the nine-foot pine tree box as she danced from one foot to the other outside the local children's hospital. Every year the Thompson family set up a Christmas tree for the children too sick to go home for the holidays. She blew the tassel from her elf hat out of her eyes and waited for the automatic door to open. This assignment was already turning out to be more *hands on* than she'd anticipated. *So much for just observing.* She caught a glimpse of herself in the glass door as they entered and sighed. Samantha would be proud. The green velvet elf hat the Thompson family insisted she wear looked ridiculous. No one had taken her protests seriously, and she'd even been forced to wear the matching hat. The ligaments in her forearm felt like they were about to tear, and her fingers were slipping from the corner of the box. She wondered how she'd gotten stuck carrying this heavy thing anyhow. *Where was Cole?* She hadn't seen him since they arrived in the parking lot. "Are we planning to put this down soon?" She called over the top of the box to Scott.

"A little further. We set up in the main cafeteria." Scott wasn't struggling under the weight.

"This way, Madison." Emma pointed the way down the hall. She skipped down the tiled hallway.

"Okay," she mumbled, straining to make it the extra remaining steps to the cafeteria.

"Here is fine." Scott gestured for her to put her side down.

She placed her end on the floor with a thud and stepped back, rubbing her throbbing arms. She would be sore tomorrow. She glanced around the cafeteria. Cole was nowhere in sight. *Typical man. Never around when there was work to do.*

The young girls unloaded bags of decorations onto the cafeteria tables, and Madison took a seat to catch her breath.

She removed her elf hat and shook her long dark hair. *Damn that thing was warm.*

"You better put your hat back on before Santa gets here." Amelia warned as she untangled a set of colored lights.

"It's a little early for San…" The words died on Madison's lips as the sound of *Ho Ho Ho* came bellowing down the hallway followed by squeals and giggles from the children.

Emma's eyes widened. "Too late he's here!" Her mouth fell open in awe as she stared at the cafeteria entrance.

Madison turned. Her eyes met Santa's, and he winked. *Oh my God! Cole?* Dressed in red velvet with a white fur trim and beard, fake belly and black shiny boots he was almost unrecognizable.

"Quick Madison, put this on before he sees you." Amelia handed her the hat.

Madison sighed and put the hat back on. Instant heat. *Cole must be sweating in that full suit.*

Scott fastened the tree in the stand and waved at Santa.

"Okay everyone, it looks like the tree is all set. Let's grab some decorations and get to work. *Ho Ho Ho.*" Cole grabbed a set of lights.

Madison remained seated as the young girls ran to join the others. She studied the scene before her, and her heart swelled. Pajama clad children laughed and danced around the tree as Santa teased and tickled them. Sadness filled her heart at the thought that this was most likely the only tree these children would see this year. The prospect of going home for most was slim. Bringing Christmas to them was their only option. Tears sprang to Madison's eyes at the good-hearted nature of the Thompson family. *The Melissa Thompson Foundation* generated cancer research funds in the millions every year, but Scott still felt it wasn't enough. His girls may be privileged, but they were far from spoiled. Their kindness and generosity proved overwhelming.

Her eyes met Cole's, and she swallowed the lump in her throat. He smiled and gestured for her to join them.

Madison hesitated. The assignment requirements were to observe, nothing more. Decorating a tree had not been in her holiday plans. Too many memories.

She bit her lip. Maybe it was time to make some new memories. After all, these children were making the best of their sad situation. Her problems paled in comparison. She grabbed a set of silver bulbs and joined the group by the tree. "Okay Santa, where should I start?" Her eyes met Cole's, and her pulse raced at the kindness she saw. She had to give him credit. It took a special kind of person to don a Santa suit. Maybe Cole Harris wasn't so bad after all. Even more reason to keep her distance.

* * * *

Cole folded the Santa suit and placed it into a duffel bag. He slid into his jeans and buttoned the top. Grabbing a hand towel, he dried the sweat from the back of his neck and bare chest. *Man that suit was hot.* He pulled his sweater over his head and raked a hand through his hair. Every year he said he wouldn't do it, and every year Scott talked him into it. In truth, it wasn't hard. He would do anything to honor his sister's memory, and the foundation was a huge contributor to the children's hospital.

He grinned as he caught sight of his reflection in the bathroom mirror. The Santa beard still hung from his chin. He tugged it off and tossed it inside the bag. He gathered his coat and camera bag and headed back toward the cafeteria.

From the doorway he could see Madison and the girls cleaning up the remainder of the loose decorations and ribbons. She laughed at something Emma said, and warmth flowed through him at the sight and sound. He'd suspected her tough exterior was only an inch thick. Underneath the cynicism was a kind-hearted, warm person. *Something*—or more likely *someone*—had ruined the holiday season for her. He suspected it was her ex-husband. Looking at her, you couldn't tell. She hummed Christmas carols as she worked.

He set up the tripod and positioned the camera. His job as Santa was done, now for the real work. Extended projects and magazine photo-shoots were the next step in his career. This assignment hadn't been a dream come true. But his portfolio would benefit from a spread in one of New York's most popular women's magazines. He snapped a few shots and smiled.

"We are about ready to head out." Scott said a moment later, hiding a yawn behind a hand. "The girls may still be going strong," he laughed, watching them twirl until they were dizzy, "but I'm exhausted."

"Okay, I'll just grab a couple more, and then pack up." Cole nodded, focusing the lens for another shot.

Scott glanced in the direction the camera pointed and grinned. "Did you take *any* of me?"

"Nope." Cole laughed. His brother-in-law knew him too well. He punched his shoulder.

"I can't say I blame you this time. She is beautiful and the girls love her."

Their eyes landed on Madison, where she sat reading a Christmas story to a group of sleepy toddlers.

"From what I've gathered so far—she isn't a fan of Christmas." Cole shrugged and dismantled the tripod.

"From what I've gathered, she isn't big on you either," Scott teased. "What did you do? Let me guess, you hit on her already."

Cole flushed. He couldn't help it if he came on too strong. He liked her. Smart, sexy and so far seemingly unattainable, what man wouldn't be attracted and challenged by her? He reached into his coat pocket and pulled out the Christmas story about the forgotten elf. "I submitted this…just to meet her." He handed the story to Scott.

Scott's mouth dropped. "This is Amelia's homework. She's been looking everywhere for this. It's due at school next week." He punched Cole playfully in the arm.

"Ow…Well, apparently it needs work." He grinned.

Scott shook his head and sighed. "I'll go get the girls. Pack it up."

"Sure thing. Just a couple more." He peered through the lens and smiled. There was something about Madison he couldn't explain, but whatever it was, it made him want to protect her, make her forget her broken heart and help her past the walls she'd built so high around herself. He suspected it would be a challenge, but he had three weeks to prove to her not all men were bad. Maybe he could convince her to give Christmas a second chance as well. Studying her smiling face from across the room, he grinned. Today was a good first step.

Chapter Three

Madison opened her laptop and sat on the hotel bed later that evening. She planned to enter the day's notes on Scott Thompson and his family and then do some long overdue writing. Her own manuscripts were neglected, with her hectic work schedule at the magazine. Thankfully, she'd yet to hear from M and M publishing regarding her recent novel submission. She lacked the time needed to devote to the editing process.

She flipped through her notebook to the scribbled notes she'd made throughout the day. While her computer loaded, she glanced outside. A light dusting of snow collected on the city below. Despite how depressing the season made her, the sight was beautiful, peaceful, magical. New York during the holidays was a city unlike any other. Her laptop login appeared, and she typed her password. She opened a new word document.

The sound of Cole's shower running in the next room distracted her, and an image of him in the Santa's suit flashed across her mind. She smiled. An image of him naked in the shower replaced the previous one, and her smile disappeared. Her cheeks flushed. She forced the image from her mind, only to have it reappear. *Dammit. Okay, he's hot. Extremely hot.* She didn't need to see the body beneath the clothes to know it was perfection. His arms were solid, and his sculpted chest refused to be contained in the white t-shirt he'd been wearing that afternoon.

"Forget about Cole and focus." She scanned her notes and typed in the information about Scott Thompson and his family.

However, despite her best efforts, images of Cole demanded her attention. His wet jet-black hair falling onto his forehead, his big muscular arms pushing it back off of his face. One occupational hazard to being a romance novelist was she envisioned things in slow motion and vividly.

She shifted on the bed and opened the file to her manuscript. *Okay time to get serious.* She tied her long hair at the base of her neck and stared at the computer screen.

Hot water trickling down the length of Cole's torso appeared.

Her pulse raced, and her cheeks flushed. *What was wrong with her? Why couldn't she shake the images of her co-worker's body? Because he is sexier than Brad Pitt, and she hasn't been with a man in three years.* She let out a deep breath. *This was ridiculous.* She heard the water shut off. *Oh thank God.*

Feeling inspiration in an area she hadn't in months, she flipped to a blank section of her manuscript. *Insert Love Scene here.* Her fingers flew across the keyboard.

Richard turned the tap to hot, and stepped inside the steaming shower. He heard the key in the front door. Mackenzie was home. Perfect timnkiyjvk...

Loud laughter from the room next door startled her. She jumped and put her hand to her chest. She shot a glare toward the wall.

She continued typing. Back space, back space, back space...*timing. The sound of her footsteps on the wooden staircase echoed throughout the house. His excitement grew with each click clack of her stilettos. An image of her sexy legs flashed behind his closed lids as the hot water trickled down his face.*

More laughter interrupted her thoughts.

How the hell was she supposed to write a love scene with him laughing like a hyena next door? Okay in fairness, it was a deep, sexy laugh, but still. She waited. Just the muted sounds of the voices on the television. She started again...

He ran his trembling hands through his wet blond hair... Blond hair? *Hmm.* She hit the search and replace function. Find *Blond* Replace With *Black. Much better.*

"Ha ha ha." Came floating through the wall.

"Okay, that's it." Madison pushed the laptop aside and swung her legs over the side of the bed. Pulling on her ugg-boot style slippers, she stood and tore open the hotel room door. Marching out into the hall, she banged on Cole's hotel room door.

"This is a surprise..."

"*What* are you laughing at?" She looked past him to the television. A familiar New York Christmas scene flashed across the screen.

"*Home Alone Two.*" He moved aside, motioning for her to come in.

She cocked her head to the side and remained in the hallway. "Seriously? What are you, twelve?"

"It's a classic." He glanced toward the screen. "This is the part where he sees the bad guys in New York." He sat on the bed, and once again gestured for her to come in.

"No, I can't. I'm working." She held the door open. "I just came over to ask you to keep the laughing to a dull roar if you could."

He didn't take his eyes off of the screen. "Sure, sorry." He gave a quick smile in her direction. He picked up the remote control and adjusted the volume.

"Thanks." She let the door close and headed back to her room. She wiggled the doorknob. *Locked. Shit.* She'd forgotten her room key. She glanced at her shorts and ugg slippered feet. She couldn't go down to the lobby of a five star hotel dressed like this. She rested her head against the door and sighed. She'd call the front desk to have one brought up. Gritting her teeth she pounded on Cole's door again.

"Change your mind?"

"No. I um…locked myself out of my room." She shifted from one foot to the other.

He smirked and leaned against the doorframe. "And you want to stay here tonight?"

"No!" Her eyes widened.

Cole laughed.

She felt foolish. Her face flushed. "Can I use your phone?" She pointed to the hotel phone on the desk.

"Sure." He moved aside to let her in.

"Thanks." She picked up the phone and hit the button for the main desk.

"Front desk."

"Hi. This is Madison Grey from room three forty-six. I locked myself out of the room, could I have a key brought up? I'd come down, but I'm in my pajamas." Heat radiated down her neck under Cole's scrutinizing gaze on her bare legs. She covered the mouthpiece. "Watch your movie." She nodded toward the television.

He laughed and turned his attention back to the television.

"No problem. We will be there shortly. Can you wait in the room you're calling from?" The desk clerk asked.

Not really. Cole, in his pajama pants and bare chest were too much. "Sure…hurry…please." Embarrassed, she replaced the receiver and turned. "They'll be here in a minute." She folded her arms across her body. A pajama party was the last thing she needed.

"No problem. Sit." He tapped the bed next to him and shuffled over to make room.

"I'm okay." She turned her attention to the screen.

Macauley Culkin ran through the streets of New York escaping the villains. Madison wished she could trade places with him. The danger of *Central Park* was nothing compared to the situation she found herself in. She shifted her weight and pulled out the desk chair and sat. Her eyes never left the screen. Better to appear engrossed in the movie than openly drooling over Cole's six-pack abs and sculpted chest. *This movie was funny.* She crossed her legs and sat back to enjoy the comedic scenes. She hadn't seen it in years.

Fifteen minutes later, she jumped at the loud knock on Cole's door.

"Your key." Cole stood and opened the door.

Madison followed.

"Here you are Ms. Grey. Sorry for the wait," the bellhop said.

"Thank you." Madison took the key and exited the room.

Cole handed the bellhop a bill.

The man smiled and tucked it into his pocket.

"I'll pay you back," Madison said.

"Don't worry about it. I'll expense it." Cole laughed. "Sure you don't want to stay and finish watching the movie?"

Madison forced herself not to look anywhere but at the cardboard key. The temptation to say *yes,* too strong. "No, thanks."

"Okay, goodnight."

"Night," she mumbled, letting herself into her room.

She sat on the bed and grabbed the laptop, her thoughts on anything but writing. *Get a grip. It's not like you've never seen a shirtless man before.* She shook her head and retyped her login on the laptop. *Not one that hot.*

She scanned what she'd written, but images of Cole's biceps and hairless chest blurred the words. She sighed.

Loud laughter floated through the thin wall followed by a, "Sorry Madison."

Madison closed the laptop and pulled back the bed sheets. She climbed into the bed and fluffed the oversized, down-filled pillows behind her back. She grabbed the remote and flipped to the program guide. *Home Alone Two* was on channel eight. *Why not? Tis the season after all.*

* * * *

Madison pulled a tan V-neck sweater over her head and smoothed her static filled flyaway hair. She grabbed her brown dress pants from the edge of the ironing board and pulled them on over her hips. She sat on the edge of the bed and reached for her shoes. The hotel room phone rang. She cringed, wondering if she should ignore it. She could claim she'd been in the shower. Cole had already texted her cell phone to invite her to join him for breakfast, and her excuses to avoid spending time with her sexy travel companion were running out. She glanced at the clock near the phone. 8:06. They were meeting the Thompson's at their family Christmas tree farm in an hour. She sighed and stared at the ringing phone. If she didn't answer, he'd come knock on her door. She picked up the receiver. "Hello."

"Madison, hi."

Madison let out a sigh of relief. *Samantha.* "Hi, Samantha." She gathered her notes, still scattered across the bed, abandoned from the night before.

"How are things going so far?" Concern filled her friend's tone.

Madison paused. *How were things going?* "Better than I thought they would." *Most honest answer.* "Of course, at this point it's just the *Christmas everywhere I look* factor I'm dealing with, but the

bachelor I met yesterday is wonderful, and his girls are adorable."
Her stomach growled. She poured a cup of coffee and grabbed a
banana chocolate chip muffin from the basket on the desk. *Eight
dollars for a muffin?* Oh well, Damian deserved a hefty travel
expense bill for sending her on this assignment.

"You sound better than the last time we spoke."

"Honestly, I've even found myself getting into the Christmas
spirit a little bit." She peeled the muffin and took a bite. *Worth
every penny of the eight dollars.*

"That's great!"

"Don't get too excited." Madison savored the muffin. "I'm not
rushing out to buy a sweater with a reindeer face on it or
anything." She picked a chocolate chip from the top of the muffin
and popped it into her mouth.

Silence greeted her on the other end.

"Samantha, tell me you're not wearing a sweater with a
reindeer face on it." She took a sip of her hot coffee and smiled.
She could get used to these travel assignments.

"It was a gift from my aunt last year."

Madison laughed.

The sound of yelling on Samantha's end on the line made her
move the receiver away from her ear. "What is that?"

"The boys. Mason is sick today, so I stayed home with him."
She lowered her voice. "I made the mistake of keeping the other
two home from daycare to have a Christmas craft day." She
covered the receiver. "Boys! Quit bickering. Mason give your
brother back the googly eyes." She yelled to her kids.

The boys were cute, but they fought often, as brothers do.
"Everything okay?"

Samantha laughed. "Oh yeah, just typical brotherly love."

"Googly eyes?"

"Candy cane reindeers—you know with pipe cleaner antlers
and googly eyes." Samantha laughed. "Never mind, I forgot who
was talking to."

"No, I know what you're talking about." Maybe the
Thompson girls might like to make those later that day. If they left
early enough, she could stop and buy the supplies on the way. She
smiled, liking the idea.

"You do?" Samantha's shock was evident.

Madison shook her head and laughed. "You know Sam, I was a child once too."

"I know…sorry you just dislike Christmas so much I figured…"

"Don't worry, I know I won't be winning any awards for Christmas spirit any time soon." But for the sake of her sanity on this trip, maybe it was best not to try so hard to avoid the festivities surrounding her. The day before had been much more enjoyable when she'd let go of her Grinch mood and participated in the events.

"Oh no, Madison. I hate to cut this short but Jake's gluing his hand to the candy cane…"

"No problem, Sam. Call me later. Give the boys a hug for me." She replaced the receiver and smiled. Her friend was incredible. She didn't know how she did it.

* * * *

"Here you go, Madison." Cole handed her a cup of steaming black coffee later that evening.

The Thompson girls decorated their freshly cut, nine foot Christmas tree, and the three adults supervised to ensure *all* the bulbs didn't end up on the bottom branches. Even without decorations, the tree was spectacular. Symmetrical and full. It had been planted on the family farm for this occasion thirty years before when Scott was a boy.

"Thank you." Madison glanced at her watch and frowned. "We should leave soon." The thought of ending their time with the family saddened her. In a few short days, she'd grown fond of them. As much as she hated to admit it, she was also growing fond of their uncle. *A little too fond of him.* He loved children, and his nieces adored him. He would make a good father. She wondered what he would be like as a husband. She flushed and looked away from his gaze.

"Madison, come help us string popcorn for the tree." Emma carried a big plastic bowl of popcorn into the living room. She set it on the floor in front of the tree and kneeled beside it. She popped a handful of the treat into her open mouth.

"Hey! Leave some for the tree." Amelia strung several needles with long lengths of thread.

Grateful for the excuse to put some distance between herself and Cole, Madison sat on the floor around the big bowl of popcorn and accepted a needle from Amelia.

Cole resumed his post behind the camera.

Madison couldn't wait to see his photos. He must have taken a hundred or more of the Thompson family that week. He refused to let her even take a peek.

Scott joined them a moment later and popped a disk into the CD player. Soon the sound of the *Chipmunks Christmas Carols* competed with a chorus of *ouches* and laughter as the group pricked their fingers with the needles.

"Uh oh, Madison, you're bleeding!" Emma's face turned white, and her eyes widened.

Blood trickled from Madison's finger. "You're right." She grabbed a tissue from the box on the end table. Blood soaked through the thin mesh. "Wow. That must have been a deep one." She laughed at the look of concern on the eight year old's face. "Don't worry, I'm okay."

"Let me take a look at that." Cole set his camera on the tripod and knelt next to her on the floor. He took her hand in his.

A ripple of electricity spiralled through Madison's core at the touch. His hands were strong, gentle and warm.

"I'm fine really. It's just a tiny dot—you won't be able to see it." Her cheeks flushed a deep shade of crimson as he examined her finger.

The two girls stopped working and watched in fascination.

"We don't like to take any chances around here, do we girls?" Cole's smile was mischievous as he winked at his nieces.

"Nope! Kiss it Uncle Cole." Emma moved closer to watch.

The older girl giggled, and Scott hid a smile behind his coffee cup.

Madison yanked her hand to free it from his grasp, but his hold tightened, preventing her escape. "Really, I'm fine."

"Just to be safe." Cole's eyes held hers as he lifted her finger to his lips.

The kiss was quick and soft. As his lips grazed the surface of her skin, a shiver vibrated through her.

She pulled her hand away and turned her attention to the girls. She fought to make light of the exchange despite her racing pulse. "That was a close one, but I think I'll be able to keep the finger." She examined the tiny dot on her shaking hand and nodded.

Emma sighed in relief

"Get back to work." Amelia shoved the string of popcorn into her sister's hand.

"Madison, we should go." Cole picked up his camera and tucked it inside the case.

"NOOOO!" Emma squealed, a frown forming on her face.

"Do you have to?" Amelia turned to Madison, disappointment evident in her tone. The two had formed a bond in their brief time together.

"Yes girls. Uncle Cole and Madison have plans tonight." Scott said.

Cole shook his head and put a finger to his lips behind Madison's back.

"I think…" Scott wore a confused look. He threw his arms up and shrugged. "Sorry Cole, I never was one for keeping secrets."

"What plans?" Madison frowned and turned to face Cole. This was the first she'd heard of any plans. Her plans for the evening included finishing the manuscript she'd given up on the night before.

Cole shrugged. "Nothing special. I have to go to my studio in the city, and I thought you'd like to come with me before we head back to the hotel. It's on the way." He picked up her coat from the back of an armchair and helped her slide into it.

"I don't know. I have work to do." Madison lifted her hair above the collar of her jacket. She *was* dying to see his work. From Samantha's praise, she suspected he was a fantastic photographer.

"Oh, come on." He rubbed her arms and turned her around to face him. "I *did* save your finger after all." He reached for the buttons on her coat.

She shot him a look through narrowed eyes and moved away from him. "I don't know…"

"I'll even treat you to one of New York's finest stale jumbo dogs I saw you drool over yesterday." Cole teased, a last attempt to persuade her.

"I was not…" Madison blushed. The smell from the street vendor's hot dog stand the day before, outside of the hospital, had indeed been tempting. She hesitated. Her size six pants fit a bit tight. "Fine." She sighed. She could diet in the New Year. "But we can't be too late." Madison made him promise. She did have work to do. Damien had emailed the night before wanting her notes on bachelor number one. She tried not to let him bother her, he was checking in on her, though she suspected he didn't treat the other staff writers the same way.

"It will only take a few minutes. I need to grab more film. I've taken more pictures, so far, than I'd planned." Cole slid into his leather jacket and wrapped his scarf around his neck.

After saying goodbye to the Thompson family, Madison and Cole climbed into his truck and arrived at his downtown studio less than fifteen minutes later. Located on the top floor of a loft style building, with windows lining one complete wall from ceiling to floor, the suite had a magnificent view of the city. "I love the view." Madison approached the window.

"That was the biggest selling feature for me." Cole nodded as he joined her at the window. "This city is incredible, especially at Christmas time. There is always a hustle and bustle down below on the streets, and it's so great to watch it from up here. Do you visit the city often?" He asked.

"No, not since the d…" *Divorce. No need to open that topic for discussion.* "Not since accepting the position at *Women's World*." She turned to admire the artwork on the walls. "These are amazing."

Her attempt at changing the subject was successful.

Cole took her from photo to photo explaining where each was taken. Photos from Europe and Japan, Tokyo and Germany lined the walls. Some were in color, and others were in black and white. The majority were scenery and architectural shots, but Madison noticed many beautiful women in some of the photos as well.

Girlfriends? None of your business.

"Just models from the photo shoots." Cole winked.

She blushed. She was so transparent. People could always read her thoughts.

"Would you like a glass of red wine?" Cole opened the mini bar fridge and took out an unopened bottle.

"Red wine goes straight to my head." Madison sat on a barstool.

"That's a *yes* then." Cole grinned as he poured a tall glass of wine and handed it to her. "To one bachelor down, four more to go." He raised his glass.

She smiled and sipped on the wine. *Pace yourself.* Maybe it would slow the usual effect of the alcohol.

"Are you from New York?" Her curiosity about him grew the more time they spent together.

"No. I'm from Florida State. I came to New York seven years ago for a week long job opportunity and never went back. You?"

"California born and raised, then I moved to Ohio to work as a freelance journalist for a human rights magazine after college. Four years ago, I was offered a full time editorial position with *The Times*, and now Staten Island is home." She didn't mention *home* was an empty, one room apartment.

"Where did you study journalism?" Cole added more wine to her glass before replacing the cork. He pulled out a barstool next to her and sat.

"Berkeley Graduate School at the University of California." Madison took a sip of wine.

"It's funny, I always thought California girls were tall blondes, not gorgeous brunettes." He brushed a stray lock of hair off of her shoulder.

Goose bumps surfaced on her skin. "I could say the same for Florida boys." *I'm flirting.* His touch had felt good. *Must be the wine.* Her skin was warm and she felt light-headed. She pushed her wine glass away. *That's enough of that.*

"Fair enough." He laughed.

Her heart raced. *Nope, it had nothing to do with the wine.* Was he getting better looking the more time she spent with him? She shook her head. *Wine. It's the wine.* She reassured herself as she glanced up at his handsome face. "Maybe we should go." Spending time alone with him was not a good idea.

Cole checked his watch and drained the contents of his glass. "Yeah, okay." He stood and removed her coat from the back of her chair.

She slid into her coat and fell off balance. *What was in that wine?*

He wrapped an arm tight around her waist to steady her and drew her into his muscular frame. "You okay?" His breath was warm on the side of her neck as he murmured into her ear.

Madison cleared her throat and took a step forward out of his embrace. "I'm fine." She swallowed hard.

He maintained his grip on her waist as she turned to face him.

"I told you the red wine would affect me." She gave a nervous laugh as he took a step toward her, closing the distance between them.

"Are you sure it's the wine?" His eyes burned into hers.

No. She lowered her chin and nodded.

He slid a hand under her chin and forced her eyes to meet his. The intensity in the ice blue eyes made her pulse race.

Why did he have to be so handsome? She fought the urge to wrap her arms around his neck.

"Madison, you are a beautiful woman." Cole traced a hand along her jaw and down the hollow of her neck. His face lowered until his forehead rested against hers.

Madison refused to raise her gaze to him. *He is your co-worker. What are you doing? What was* he *doing?* She couldn't let this assignment become any more complicated. She took a deep breath and broke free of his grasp. "We should go." With shaky hands, she busied herself with the buttons on her coat.

Cole's face fell as his arms dropped to his sides. "You're right. It's getting late. Just give me a second to grab more film, then we can head back to the hotel."

Madison grabbed his arm as he turned away. "Cole."

"Yeah?" His expression was hopeful.

"You still owe me a hot dog." She let his arm fall back to his side.

Cole laughed and shook his head. "Yes I do, little lady."

Chapter Four

Bachelor number two, Nathan Harper, was an overnight success in the fashion industry. His modern designs for *Gucci* appeared overnight, and his overwhelming success followed suit. Designer shoes and handbags with the *NH* logo were this year's rage all over New York. Madison had to admit she'd been tempted more than once to purchase one of his big ticket items. His designs were practical as well as stylish, and his shoes were comfortable to wear for more than an hour at a time, a rare find for high heels.

A Texas native, his southern drawl combined with his dark good looks only helped to increase Nathan's popularity among his female followers. *GQ Magazine* had named him the Most Successful Bachelor of 2010. Reportedly single, he was linked to many short-lived relationships with the runway models he worked with.

"I'll be right with you." Nathan turned and called to them as they entered the five-star hotel ballroom where he directed stick thin models down a t-shaped runway.

"Take your time." Madison smiled and waved. Removing her gloves she shoved them into her coat pockets. She scanned the room. Elegantly dressed tables of six were set up and placed around the runway to allow ample viewing of the fashions on display that evening.

"So, about last night in my studio…" Cole shouted above the sound of hip-hop music coming from a large speaker above their heads.

"Nothing happened." Madison shook her head and refused to meet his gaze. But something almost had. She resolved not to get that close to him again.

"I beg to differ. We almost kissed." Cole gave her a pointed look.

Madison scoffed. "But we didn't." She unbuttoned her coat and removed her scarf.

"We should have." Cole moved to stand in front of her.

"We won't." She met his gaze. A stupid mistake, that's all it was. She refused to let it happen again. They were co-workers. She was more professional than this. So what if he was sexy as hell. The problem was he knew it. She refused to be another notch on his belt. "Shouldn't you be taking a picture of something?" She moved around him as Nathan approached.

"*Women's World Quarterly*, welcome to the madness." Nathan laughed as he extended a hand to Madison, then Cole, "Nice to meet you both. Please bear with me for a while, I have to make sure my newest designs are featured at various points throughout the show, and then I am done for today." He ran a hand through his wavy short dark hair.

"Your designs are fabulous." Madison smiled. Samantha would be so jealous. She had been green with envy when Madison had told her the bachelor line-up.

"Thank you. I grew up in a house full of women who constantly complained of sore feet after a long day in heels or purses too small to hold all of their accessories." He explained. "My inspiration came from them for this new winter line."

The next model approached, and Nathan turned his attention back to the runway.

Madison's eyes narrowed. There was something familiar about the strawberry blonde with the thin lips and cat-like eyes. *Where had she seen her before?*

"Cole! How great to see you!" The young girl broke her stiff form as she arrived at the end of the runway. "I didn't know you were photographing the show. The girls will be so excited, we haven't seen you since that bikini shoot last summer in Maui."

Ah ha! The Maui photos on his studio wall. Madison turned to look at Cole, eyebrows raised, an amused smile on her face. *Someone was popular with the women.*

"Oh no—I'm here as a journalistic photographer with *Women's World Quarterly* to take photos of Nathan." His face and neck flushed a deep crimson.

"Looks like someone has a way with the ladies." Nathan slapped Cole on the back.

"It's not like that." Cole shrugged as he looked back and forth between Nathan and Madison, shaking his head.

Madison smiled at his obvious discomfort. She folded her arms across her thin frame.

"Maybe I'll stop by your studio sometime. I'd love to take new shots for my portfolio." The girl winked at him and turned.

Cole flushed a deeper shade of red. "Anytime," he mumbled, studying his feet.

"Hey girls, that sexy photographer from our shoot in Maui is here." The girl yelled as she reached backstage.

Nathan and Madison laughed.

Cole rolled his eyes.

"As I was saying, once I'm done here I have some Christmas shopping to do, and I need you two to come along. I would love a woman's opinion on something." Nathan winked at Madison.

"I would love that." Shopping was something she could do. Though she suspected Nathan knew much more about today's fashion than she did.

Cole looked less impressed, but shrugged in agreement.

"Great, give me another ten minutes or so, and I'll be right with you guys." Nathan disappeared backstage.

Cole turned to Madison, "Seriously Madison, those girls are just…"

"Why are you explaining yourself to me? I'm just a co-worker, nothing more." She gave him a pointed look. "*Nothing* happened between us. Nothing is *happening* between us." She shrugged.

"Not yet." Cole grinned.

"Not ever."

"We'll see."

* * * *

Tiffany's was abuzz with shoppers. The New York store was the biggest of all of their high-end accessory locations, boasting three floors of jewelry. Entering the building, Madison scanned the showroom. Not another woman in the store. *Figures.* Dozens of men however formed long lines at each of the cash registers.

"So, what are we looking for?" Cole asked Nathan, "Earrings, a necklace?"

Someone was in a hurry to leave the store. Madison smirked. *So jewelry made him uncomfortable. Or was it the idea of commitment?* She shook her head. *What did she care?*

"Actually, I'm looking for an engagement ring. I'm planning to ask Becca to marry me." Nathan beamed.

Madison fought to hide her surprise. She'd read somewhere Nathan had been dating supermodel, Becca Sambura, but the media had always pegged them as an *on again/off again romance*, and Madison hadn't thought they were serious about the relationship. "That's wonderful. Congratulations!" She forced a smile. The idea of marriage was not one she liked to entertain. Despite the vows and promises of long lasting commitment they ended in the blink of an eye. She bit her tongue. A man in love wouldn't appreciate her negative opinion of the subject.

"Great! Let's get started. Engagement rings are on the third floor." Cole surprised them both.

Madison turned with a questioning look. *He'd been here before? When?*

"What?" He shrugged. "I helped Scott try to find an engagement ring for Melissa."

They climbed the beautiful, winding staircase to the third floor, the busiest section in the entire store. Men crowded the showcases demanding to see one ring after another. The clerks only saw dollar signs as they displayed the unending selection of diamonds and explained their warrantees and buy back policies to the confused looking men. Many brought reinforcement, but the sidekicks looked just as lost among the glitter.

"Look at all of those poor schmucks." Cole chuckled. He tucked his hands deep into his pockets and rocked back and forth on his heels. An amused smile spread across his face as he studied the scene before them.

"Not a fan of marriage?" Madison shot him a curious look.

He shrugged. "Just don't know if it's for me, that's all."

"I see." She could understand. Marriage definitely hadn't been good for *her*.

Nathan slapped Cole on the back. "Be careful buddy. I used to say the same thing until I met Becca. Now I can't imagine my life without her."

Madison gave a polite smile. She didn't remind Nathan, the tabloids suggested they'd broken up three times already that year. *Maybe the media had it wrong.* Looking at Nathan's excited face, he certainly appeared eager to marry the model.

"Though I guess I'm not being unique by proposing at Christmas huh?" Nathan joked as they made their way through the thick crowd of people to the first display case. Cluster diamond sets shone through the spotless glass.

"So, do you know if she likes clusters or solitaires? White or yellow gold?" Cole scanned the display case.

Nathan looked puzzled. "I don't know." Nathan examined the rings. "I think I may be in way over my head here."

Madison suspected he was right if the media was right about Becca Sambura. She didn't comment, instead pretending to scan the rings.

"No problem. Let's take it one step at a time." Cole turned to Nathan. "A solitaire is one diamond, and a cluster is a set of diamonds. Yellow gold is traditional and white gold is popular right now." Cole moved to a second display case and pointed out the differences for Nathan.

"I definitely think white gold. Becca is anything but traditional, and I think she would prefer a cluster. The more diamonds the better, right?" He asked Madison.

Her eyes widened. *Don't ask me.* At the time of her engagement Kurt could have proposed with a twist tie, and she would have said *yes.* She shot a look to Cole.

The *ring expert* answered for her. "Don't worry I got this," he whispered. He turned to Nathan. "Not necessarily, with a solitaire, you can choose a large diamond. With clusters, many smaller diamonds occupy the same space."

Nathan nodded. "Okay…Solitaire it is." He looked grateful for Cole's assistance.

Madison hung back and watched in silence as they moved from display case to display case, discussing the rings. Cole was cute in his attempt to be helpful. He surprised her. Maybe she'd been too quick to judge him. That didn't mean she would be kissing him anytime soon. *Or ever.*

"Can I help you two find something?" A salesman approached the two men.

"We're looking for an engagement ring." Nathan beamed.

"So far, we've decided on a solitaire and white gold." Cole chimed in.

The salesman looked between the two men, a puzzled look on his thin white face. He shrugged. "We usually don't see a man wearing an engagement ring, but why not right?" He smiled. "So which of you will be wearing the band?" He held a ring sizer in his hand.

"Oh no, you misunderstood..." Nathan held his hands up in protest.

Cole moved away, shaking his head.

Madison laughed at the scene and covered her mouth as the three men turned to look at her. The look of desperation on the faces staring at her was too funny for words.

Cole pulled her over to the counter, refusing to let go of her arm once she was there.

"So, *this* is the special lady?" The salesman frowned.

"Oh no...I'm not." Madison shook her head, horrified at the suggestion. She doubted she'd ever be *the special lady* again.

"I'm confused." The salesman leaned against the counter.

"*I'm* buying a ring for my *girlfriend.* These are my friends." Nathan gestured to Cole and Madison.

"Okay, that's better. White gold and a solitaire, you say?" The clerk wiped at the fingerprints they'd left on the display case.

Nathan nodded.

"Let's find that perfect ring." The clerk led Nathan to the solitaire case.

Madison looked at Cole and laughed again. His face still wore a terrified expression.

Nathan disappeared through the crowd, leaving them alone.

"What's so funny?" Cole reached toward her and tickled her ribs.

"You two." Madison swatted his hand away. "How do you know so much about rings anyway?"

"I told you. Scott dragged me to every jewelry store in New York to find the perfect ring for Melissa. I paid attention, and I learned a lot. Too much." Cole traced a hand along the edge of a display case.

"So did he find it?" Madison asked. "This *perfect* ring."

"Not here or any of the other thousand jewelry stores he dragged me to. He couldn't find anything traditional enough for Melissa. Then later that day, his mom called to say his grandmother had passed away and had left him a few things in her will. Her engagement ring and wedding band set were among them. The rings had my sister written all over them, and she loved that they were a family heirloom. Amelia and Emma will get them one day." Cole's expression was sad.

Madison's heart went out to him. She couldn't imagine losing a loved one to an illness. She resisted the urge to touch his arm. Better to keep as much distance between them as possible. These softer sides of her travel companion were more dangerous than his advances.

Cole stopped and pointed to a ring in a display case. "That ring would look beautiful on your finger."

Madison refused to acknowledge the ring he pointed to. She shook her head. "I'm not in the market for an engagement ring." She shuddered at the thought.

"Maybe not yet…" he whispered. His breath lingered on the back of her neck.

She moved away from him. "Never." Or more accurately, never *again*.

"You say that a lot." He smirked and touched the tip of her nose.

She swatted his hand away. "And I mean it."

"Hey guys, I think I found it." Nathan yelled from a few feet away.

Grateful for the distraction, Madison joined Nathan by the display case. Cole followed.

The clerk beamed as he waited their approval of his suggestion.

"Do you think she will like it?" Nathan held a two-carat diamond for their inspection.

Madison gasped at the price tag. She swallowed hard and nodded.

"It's perfect," Cole said.

For that price, it had better be.

"Great. I'll go pay for it, and then we're out of here." Nathan followed the clerk to the register.

"Becca's a model right?" Cole lowered his voice and leaned toward Madison.

Madison nodded. "Yeah, why?"

Cole placed a hand on the small of her back as they descended the crowded staircase to the main floor. He stopped when they reached the front door. "That two carat rock will probably be the heaviest part of her." Cole grinned leading the way out of the store.

* * * *

Cole wasn't wrong in his assessment of Becca Samura. Five foot eleven and weighing no more than a hundred pounds, the girl was beautiful with curly red hair reaching her waist and slanted hazel eyes.

Cole glanced at his watch. 11:16. He drummed his fingers against Nathan's dining room table. "What could possibly be taking her so long?" He hissed at Madison. They'd been waiting for Becca to get ready for almost an hour.

"Shh," Madison put her finger to her lips. She resumed typing on her iPad.

Cole stood and paced the living room.

Nathan had invited the two of them to join them at the spa that afternoon. He planned to propose that evening and wanted to make sure Becca was refreshed and relaxed. Cole wasn't thrilled at the prospect of a spa day, but he couldn't complain about a free massage.

"Nathan, could you zip me?" Becca emerged from the bedroom in a one-piece black jumper.

She's wearing that *to a spa?*

"Gladly." Nathan helped her with the zipper, placing a trail of kisses along her long neck as he did.

Cole rolled his eyes. *Oh come on.* He'd like to be doing the same thing to Madison, but no one needed to see it. Public displays of affection were not his *thing.*

Madison hid a giggle behind her hand. She tucked the iPad into her purse and stood.

"Okay, I'm ready. Let's go. Dahlia hates it when I am late." Becca clapped her hands.

Cole suspected Becca was late for a lot of things. *High maintenance women.* He shook his head as he wrapped his scarf around his neck. He didn't see the appeal. He preferred a natural beauty, like Madison. Her alarm went off in the room next to his every morning at eight, and she was always waiting for him in the lobby less than an hour later. Looking beautiful as ever. *That*, he could appreciate.

Becca's brand new black *Audi R8* awaited them in her parking space in the underground parking garage. Nathan uncovered the car and opened the passenger side for Becca, and then opened the driver side door for Cole and Madison. He leaned in and pulled the driver side seat back. He waited for them to climb in.

Cole looked at Madison and down at his tripod and camera bags. He didn't travel light. The backseat of the car was just big enough to fit the two of them.

"Maybe we should take the truck and meet you two at the spa." Madison ran a hand along the beautiful black exterior. She looked disappointed.

The smell of the new leather escaped from the open door.

"Nonsense, there's plenty of room. Y'all *have* to experience this car. I bought it for her for her birthday, but she refuses to drive it herself." Nathan laughed.

"We're going to be late." Becca huffed from inside the car.

Cole cringed. Her voice had a nail on a chalkboard effect. *How could Nathan deal with that whiny sound?* He preferred Madison's voice—rich, silky and incredibly sexy.

"Well?" Madison asked. Her eyes begged him to say *yes*.

Funny, he hadn't pegged her for a fast car kind of girl. "Why not?" Cole shrugged his shoulders and climbed into the backseat placing his tripod on the back windowsill of the car and securing his backpack in the tiny space between his feet on the floor. *Not bad.*

Madison climbed in next to him and almost sat on his lap. These cars were not designed with the comfort of the backseat passengers in mind.

Cole smiled, grateful for the tiny, confined space. He could smell Madison's hair, and he took a deep breath. The distinct smell of peppermint filled the space between them, and he resisted the urge to kiss the top of her head. Their shoulders touched, and each time the car took a sharp turn, she fell against him. Her hand brushed his leg on the seat, and he fought the urge to wrap an arm around her, drawing her closer. She'd made it clear, his advances were unwelcome, but the look in her eyes the night before in his studio told a different story. Keeping his hands and lips off of her would be a challenge.

Despite the driving speed, they *were* late, and Becca pouted when she learned Dahlia had gotten tired of waiting for her, and had taken a different client. She was reassigned to a young girl named Anna, who looked nervous while Becca made demands, as they disappeared down the hall.

Cole, Madison and Nathan were ushered down the hallway toward the dressing rooms. The spa hostess handed them big, terry cloth bathrobes and slippers to change into. The spa was spectacular with its ancient Egyptian theme and décor and dimly lit hallways. The tranquil sound of running waterfalls had the desired soothing effect, and the aroma of jasmine in the air invigorated the senses. Their Christmas décor consisted of a few decorated white Jesse trees in various corners of the spa.

"So, what's the deal with you two?" Nathan asked when they were alone in the waiting area. Madison had yet to emerge from the women's changing room.

"Who?" Cole avoided Nathan's eyes. *Was his interest in Madison that transparent?*

"You and our beautiful little journalist." Nathan leaned back against the plush cushions of the velvet armchair.

"Nothing." Cole shrugged. It was true. So far, she'd fought off his advances. Her guard didn't seem to be coming down as quick as he'd assumed or hoped it might. Working for a woman's affection was foreign to him, but he suspected she was worth the effort.

"Whatever, man. There is so much sexual tension between the two of you, it makes Becca and I look like an old married couple already." Nathan took a sip of his lemon water. He grimaced and looked at the glass. "Could use a shot of vodka." He laughed and set the glass aside.

Other people could sense the tension between them? "As you said, she's beautiful, who wouldn't be attracted to her, but we're just co-workers." *For now.*

Madison emerged from the changing room and laughed as she joined them.

"What's so funny?" Cole's eyes rested a little too long on her bare legs. *Man, they were sexy. How would they feel wrapped around him? God, he hoped their working relationship changed soon.* He didn't know how much longer he'd be successful in keeping his hands to himself.

"You two." Madison took a seat next to Cole on the couch. "If only the sales clerk at Tiffany's could see you two lovebirds now." She reached for a grape.

The men laughed at the memory of the clerk and Cole shuddered.

"Cole?" A massage therapist appeared and glanced between the two men.

Nathan pointed to Cole. "You're up buddy. Enjoy."

Cole stood and followed the petite woman into the therapy room.

"I'll let you disrobe and climb under this top sheet. I'll knock before entering." She turned on a soothing sounds CD and dimmed the lighting in the room before exiting.

Cole nodded.

The woman closed the door behind her.

Cole disrobed and climbed onto the soft, padded massage table. He rested his face in the headrest and wiggled his hips on the table into a comfortable position. *Thank you Women's World Quarterly.* So far this assignment felt nothing like work. He relaxed his shoulders and let his arms rest at his sides. His legs and feet sank into the table.

Madison's voice in the room next to his came through the thin wall.

He stiffened. *How the hell was he supposed to relax knowing she was disrobing in the next room?* Images of his sexy travel companion lying naked on the massage table clouded his head. *Damn, what a lucky massage therapist.*

* * * *

"Should I get down on one knee in the restaurant or slide it across the table?" Nathan stopped pacing his living room and turned to Madison and Cole. That evening, he'd made reservations to take Becca to dinner at her favorite Mexican restaurant in Manhattan, though it was still up for debate, whether or not she did in fact eat.

Madison and Cole sat on his couch and watched him go back and forth.

"I think he's asking you." Madison poked Cole in the shoulder. She'd been discounted as a valued authority on the subject after she'd suggested a blue tie, instead of a red one and had been outvoted by the two men. The whole situation was hilarious. So far, he'd tried several *proposal attempts*, which Cole continued to refuse.

"I'm not sure." Cole paused. "I'm just not feeling it. Maybe try the knee again." Cole sat ready, his head high, shoulders back in his best impression of Becca.

Madison watched the two with amusement.

"Oh forget it. It's getting late." Nathan picked up his watch from the counter and snapped it in place. He grabbed his sports coat. "I have to go. Make yourselves comfortable, and when we get back we'll have a drink to celebrate. *If* she says *yes*. Oh no. What if she says *no*?" Panic crept into his voice, and he paced again, biting his lower lip.

"She won't." Madison stood and took him by the shoulders. His pacing made her dizzy.

"Cole did."

Madison struggled to supress a giggle. "Did you really want to marry Cole?" She cocked her head to the side.

The tension in Nathan's shoulders disappeared. "I guess not."

"Hey! What's wrong with me? You could do much worse you know." Cole's eyes burned into Madison's.

Madison glanced at her watch, breaking the gaze. "You're going to be late." She pushed Nathan toward the door. "Go. Good luck."

He leaned and gave her a quick hug. "Thanks." He waved to Cole and disappeared into the hall.

Once the door closed behind him, Madison rejoined Cole on the couch. She sat and tucked her legs beneath her. A yawn escaped her lips. She'd been lazy and relaxed since the massage.

"So, do you think that red headed terror will say *yes*?" Cole leaned against the arm of the couch.

"She's not that bad." She shook her head. *It was a lie*. The truth was, Madison couldn't understand what a terrific guy like Nathan saw in a woman like Becca, aside from the obvious fact she was beautiful. After their massages, they'd waited an additional forty-five minutes for her to emerge from the changing room. In the meantime, her massage therapist emerged in tears, claiming if she ever had to work on her again, she would quit. Nathan had been sympathetic toward the girl, giving her what Madison could only assume was a very large tip. The tears dried the moment the bills were tucked into her pocket.

Becca had claimed to be hungry, and they'd driven an hour to the only raw food restaurant outside of the city. Cole had refused the food with a look of disgust, and Nathan had promised him a hamburger once they arrived back to his place. Becca had picked at her raw veggie and fish platter, and Madison struggled to enjoy a salad, feeling Becca's disapproving, and scrutinizing gaze when she dared to add salad dressing.

"Oh, come on. She looked at your salad dressing as if it was the cause of obesity." Cole shook his head and laughed. He stretched an arm out behind her on the couch.

"But you think she's beautiful at least." Madison studied her fingernails. Cole spent most of his time with women as beautiful as Becca. She couldn't understand why he wasn't dating one. *Or many*.

Cole hesitated. "She's…photogenic. Like most of the women I work with on photo-shoots. She looks wonderful with her makeup on and every strand of fiery hair is in place, but spend five minutes with her and that beauty fades. She isn't the kind of woman who looks beautiful lying in the snow, with her arms and legs flailing about, making a snow angel." Cole moved closer to her on the couch.

Madison flushed, and her pulse quickened. *Could he look any sexier?* His jeans hugged his muscular thighs, and his sweater fit tight across his chest and arms. She didn't trust herself to meet his gaze. *How did he have such an effect on her?* Since her divorce, she'd found herself the source of many men's attention but never had she been attracted to one as she was to Cole.

"By the way," Cole placed a hand under her chin and turned her face toward him, "I hope you didn't mean what you said yesterday about never kissing me." He placed a hand on her knee and leaned forward, his face inches from hers, forcing her to look at him.

I can't breathe. Madison tugged at the neck of her turtleneck. Her leg quivered under his touch. *Could he feel her trembling?* Anticipation mounted for a kiss she knew was coming, yet defenseless to prevent. She swallowed hard. *Was it hot in here*?

Cole licked his lips and lowered his head, tilting her chin upward to meet him.

Madison's hands pressed against his chest, but she didn't push him away. Instead, she clutched his sweater as her thoughts conflicted with the passion cursing through her body.

BZZZZ. Cole's cell phone vibrated in his jeans pocket.

Madison jumped and moved away from him. She took a deep breath. *Oh my God, that was close.* She tugged at the neck of her turtleneck and placed a hand to her flushed cheeks.

"Damn it," Cole muttered as he reached into his pocket and removed the vibrating phone. He glanced at the caller I.D. "It's Nathan."

"Answer it." Madison nodded toward the ringing phone. *Dammit that phone had the worse timing? Or the best?* She couldn't decide. Disappointment mixed with relief over the interruption. She stood to distance herself from him and to calm her quickened heartbeat.

"Hey Nathan, what's up?" Irritation at the interruption was evident in Cole's terse voice.

Madison folded her arms and leaned against the doorframe to the living room.

"Sure, don't worry. Give us twenty minutes." Cole said. He too had stood and paced back and forth the kitchen. He hung up the phone and turned to Madison. "He forgot the ring." He rolled his eyes.

"Are you serious?" She shook her head in disbelief. *After all that worrying and preparing, how had he done something as stupid as that?*

"Yes, and he sounds close to a panic attack. He said he left it on his bedside table. I'll grab it while you put on your coat." Cole disappeared into the bedroom.

Madison grabbed her coat from the back of the chair and tossed it over her arm. Still hot from their exchange, she longed for the cool fresh air outside.

Cole emerged from the bedroom seconds later, ring in hand. "Here it is. Shall we?" Cole opened the door and waited for her to exit. "Oh, and don't worry, I'm not forgetting about that kiss," he whispered.

Madison locked the door and jiggled the knob. "I don't know what you're talking about." The moment had passed. She was determined not to let the temptation occur again. *What happened to her resolve whenever they found themselves in a situation alone together? Why was she so helpless against his charm and gentle persuasion?* In three years, no other man had been able to weaken her resolve. She would just make sure they weren't alone together often.

"I'll be sure to remind you." Cole grabbed her hand and kissed her palm.

She didn't doubt he would. She was in trouble.

Jennifer Snow

Chapter Five

Madison yawned as she rode the elevator to the hotel lobby the next morning. She didn't get paid enough to be up this early. She wrapped her scarf around her neck and leaned her head against the elevator wall, closing her eyes. Nathan had a promotional photo shoot this morning, in *Central Park,* with the representatives of the accessories division of *Gucci.* His new collection of shoes and purses were being featured in their upcoming spring issue, hitting store shelves in March. While Cole had raved all evening about being an observer on the set, she was less than thrilled at the prospect. The day was sunny and bright, but she wasn't fooled. The morning news had announced an expected high temperature for the day of fourteen degrees. Even in her warmest layers, Madison experienced a chill as the elevator doors opened in the lobby.

Cole waited for her on a bench in the elevator lobby. His smile was wide as she approached.

Wow, someone was excited this morning.

"Good morning." Cole stood and handed her a *Starbucks* cup.

"No, *good* would have been at eight. Why do they insist on doing photo-shoots at five o'clock?" Nathan had warned them it would be an early morning, but five a.m.? Nothing should be happening this early except sleep. She accepted the coffee cup and took a big lifesaving gulp. The thick, creamy liquid stuck in her throat. She gulped. "Disgusting!" She grimaced. "What is that?" She lifted the lid to peek inside the cup.

"Eggnog latte." Cole grinned at her. "I take it you don't like it?" He laughed.

"How could anyone drink this?" She scanned the hotel lobby for the nearest garbage can and the *Starbucks*.

Cole took the cup from her and handed her a different one. "Relax, I was kidding. *Here* is your coffee."

Madison hesitated until the familiar aroma drifted from the cup. She took a sip, savouring the rich taste. The champagne the night before hadn't been a good idea, given the early morning, but she hadn't been able to refuse the happy newly engaged couple. Her head ached, one look outside at the bundled people passing by the frosted windows, and she moaned. *This assignment was more trouble than it was worth. Keep thinking about your future with the magazine.*

"There's Nathan." Cole nodded toward the entrance. He grabbed his camera and tripod and set off for the door.

Madison braced herself for the cold, tucking her head deeper into the collar of her coat and followed him out to Nathan's *Hummer*. The wind took her breath away as she waited for Cole to open the passenger side door.

He helped her up into the large vehicle then climbed into the back seat behind her.

She shivered as a blast of heat hit her feet.

"Good morning, you two. Sorry about the early rise." Nathan pulled the *Hummer* onto the street.

"No problem. We're looking forward to the shoot." Cole looked like a kid waiting for Santa.

Nathan laughed. "Maybe you are, but Madison looks like she could have used more sleep." He glanced in her direction and patted her arm.

Madison gave a weak smile. "I am tired, but this will be fun." She took another gulp of her cooling coffee and leaned her head against the seat. Content to let the two men chat about the shoot, her mind wandered, as she stared out the window. *Fifth Avenue* was quiet in the early hour before dawn, rare for the busy street. Soon it would be full of people, scurrying to their day jobs or holiday shopping. The street would come alive with glittering holiday lights and extravagant window displays in the department stores. The sound of Christmas music playing in the cafes and restaurants would drift through the opening doors. Escaping the festive sights and sounds was a challenge every year and made her heart ache. Despite the time since their separation, forgetting about Kurt and the divorce continued to be hard, and the holidays reminded her of the loneliness she fought every day. She closed her eyes and took a deep breath.

"Here we are." Nathan said, breaking into her thoughts moments later. He turned the *Hummer* into the park.

Security guards flagged them inside a barricade and motioned to the parking area.

Nathan nodded in thanks.

"Wow, look at the amount of people on set." Cole's eyes shone with excitement.

Madison was impressed. Four cameramen and their assistants worked setting up additional lighting and backdrops. Models stood under a large white tent, wrapped in big, bulky winter coats and blankets to stay warm. Security guards milled about the perimeter of the park. Madison hadn't realized so much work or so many people were involved in the creation of the ads she red-inked every quarter for the magazine.

Nathan led the way through the crowd to introduce them to the *Gucci* executives. Three men in suits and overcoats huddled together over a laptop, reviewing the photo shoot line up and making last minute changes to the rotation.

"Nathan, hi." Erik Johnson, a *Gucci* executive shook Nathan's hand.

"Erik, this is Madison Grey and Cole Harris from *Women's World*." Nathan accepted a cup of coffee from one of the assistants. "Thank you." He smiled.

Erik turned to Madison and Cole. "Welcome. It's nice to meet you both. Cole, Nathan tells us you are a very talented photographer, and I hear you've worked with some of our regular models before. They speak highly of you as well." He winked.

I bet they do. Madison shifted her eyes and shoved her hands into her pockets. *How had she forgotten gloves?* She would freeze to death out here, if the shoot lasted very long.

"Here is my business card, we're always looking for new talent." Erik handed his card to Cole.

Cole's face lit up. "Seriously? Thank you." He tucked the card into his back pocket. "Is it okay to take a few shots of Nathan at work?"

"Sure, no problem." Erik took a sip of his coffee.

"Where should I set up, so as not to interfere with the other cameras?" Cole looked around them.

"Come with me, I'll show you." Another executive offered.

The two disappeared.

Madison danced on the spot, trying to keep warm. *How long would this take anyway? Maybe she wouldn't be forced to stay for the full shoot.*

"We have a major problem people." A thin, short man appeared behind them.

"Something was bound to go wrong." Erik remained calm. "Let's hear it."

"Anya called on her mobile to say she is stuck in a traffic jam on the *Brooklyn Bridge,* and she won't be able to make it." His tone was frantic as he threw his arms into the air. He paced back and forth.

Erik put a hand out to stop the pacing. "Someone else can wear her sets." He shrugged.

"Not possible. We had to special order her shoes. She's the only six foot woman in the world with size six feet." The wardrobe assistant shook his head.

Madison stifled a giggle at the duress she heard in his voice. *So, a pair of shoes wouldn't make it into the shoot. What was the big deal?*

"This isn't funny." The assistant shot her an annoyed look. "Anya was page three. *All* of page three. Who's supposed to fill page three?" His tone grew shrill as he continued. He rested his chin on his hand and studied the ground.

Madison turned to slip away. The last thing she needed was to cause the irate little man to throw a tantrum. She wondered if anyone would notice if she slipped into the heated gazebo next to the ice rink.

"Wait a sec," the assistant said.

"Huh?" She pointed to herself and looked around. "Are you talking to me?"

He nodded and gestured for her to come closer. "What size feet do you have?"

"I'm sorry?" Madison was afraid of where this question was leading.

"The... size... of... your... feet. What is it?"

She hesitated. "Um..."

The assistant bent and grabbed her foot.

"Hey!" She pulled her foot away from him. "Six, six and a half, if I'm wearing boots."

Cole had returned and watched the scene with a grin.

Madison glared at him. *What did he find so amusing?*

"Fantastic. Hurry, come with me." The assistant tugged on the corner of her sleeve, dragging her in the direction of the wardrobe tent.

"Oh, no way." *Like hell this was happening.* "There's a misunderstanding. I'm here as a journalist from *Women's World Quarterly*. I'm not a model." Madison planted her feet and yanked her arm away.

The assistant rolled his eyes and tapped his foot on the ground.

"You could be one," Cole whispered, sneaking up on her.

"I'm not." Her eyes narrowed as she hissed at him. Turning to the executives she forced a smile, and said, "I'm sorry, but I can't." She could hear Damian now. He would be furious about her modeling for another magazine campaign. The idea was ridiculous. She refused to do it. She folded her arms across her chest and shook her head.

"Madison, could I talk to you for a moment?" Nathan pulled her aside.

"We don't have time for this," the assistant whined.

"One second." Nathan held up one finger. "Madison, since you're not on the payroll as a model, this wouldn't be considered a conflict of interest with *Women's World*, if that's what you're worried about." He lowered his voice.

"That's a big part of it, but also I have no idea how to model. I wouldn't have the slightest…" She gave a nervous laugh.

"Also, I'm not sure if you know this, but the models get to keep whatever they wear here today. The same rule will apply for you." Nathan cut her off mid protest, tempting her.

Madison struggled with the idea. She wasn't here to be showcased in a magazine wearing *Gucci*. She was a professional journalist. On the other hand, she had been eyeing his new collection for months, and Samantha would love a Nathan Harper purse for Christmas. She would never hear the end of it, if she refused. *Dammit, she was going to do it.* She sighed. "Fine, I'll do it." *This assignment would be the death of her.*

"Great, thank you." Nathan looked relieved as he kissed her hand. "She's all yours," he called to the assistant.

"Wonderful." The assistant rolled his eyes as he led Madison to the tent. He handed her several pairs of shoes to try on and nodded in approval when they fit. The matching purses were spectacular, and the price tag would be the equivalent to a month's salary for her. Next he handed her a red velvet gown and reached to unzip her coat.

She slapped his hand away. "I've got it."

"Fine, whatever. Just be quick, and then wait here Mary."

"It's *Madison*."

"What is?" He looked confused.

"My name." Madison removed her coat.

"Not today. I've already told the photographer your name is *Mary*. So today you are *Mary*." He stormed off.

Sighing, she gathered the dress and her accessories and disappeared behind a dressing screen. Thankful for the little space heater, she undressed and slipped into the gown as fast as she could. She groaned at her reflection in the full-length mirror. The dress was tight, revealing every curve. With the way she'd been eating so far on this trip, it surprised her that it fit at all.

A makeup artist poked her head around the side of the dressing screen. "Erik asked me to touch up your makeup. Is that okay?" The young woman smiled.

Did she have a choice? "Of course. Is there a way to make me look less terrified?" Madison stood still as the woman applied a pressed powder to her crimson cheeks. They could apply layers of makeup, and she still wouldn't look like these other women.

"Ah, you'll be fine once you're out there." The woman applied bright red lipstick to Madison's full lips. "Done." She smiled with approval and disappeared.

Madison checked her reflection. *Wow, what had she used on her face?* She touched her forehead in amazement. Every last line was smooth, and her skin tone looked flawless. She had to get the name of that concealer.

She grabbed a thick blanket and stood in the covered waiting area with the professional models as they each took their place in front of various backdrops. The photographer gave them little direction. They moved from one pose to another, holding each one, and then gliding into the next one with grace and ease. *What was she thinking? She couldn't do that. Not even something remotely close to that.* Her chest hurt. *Was it too late to back out?*

Cole and Nathan watched from the sidelines, and Cole smiled at her when he noticed her standing in the entryway of the sheltered area. He waved and gave a *thumbs up* sign.

Great. She was going to make a fool out of herself in front of everyone on the set, and he had a front row seat. *Why had she agreed to this?* She looked around her for an escape. No one guarded the back entry of the tent.

"Mary, you're up." The assistant poked his head inside the tent.

Too late.

Madison removed the warm blanket from around her shoulders, and stepped out from the shelter of the tent. Goose bumps covered the surface of her skin, and the cold wind whipped through the thin fabric of the dress. *How had the others stopped themselves from shivering with chattering teeth as they posed in this frigid air?*

Cole's gaze never left her as she stood in front of the first camera. He took in the tight, low cut dress, bare thighs exposed through the slit and delicate thin ankles before returning to meet her eyes. She flushed despite the cold. She remembered his promise the night before about kissing her, and his eyes revealed he wanted to do just that. *Right now.* Panic crept up the back of her neck. *Maybe this wasn't worth the free shoes after all.*

"Okay Mary, let's get started." The photographer poised, ready to shoot.

Madison sighed. *Please God, let me get through this.*

The minutes passed like seconds until the photographer announced they were done. *That was it? That wasn't so bad.* She rushed back inside the sheltered area and changed out of the gown and back into her coat and dress boots. She shivered as she hung the gown on a hanger and handed it to the wardrobe assistant.

"You did great." The young girl smiled.

"Thank you." Madison appreciated the lie. The photographer had taken at least fifty different shots, hopefully he'd be able to find enough to fill page three.

Cole waited outside the tent when she emerged. "You were incredible." He stood in front of her and pulled her scarf tighter around her neck.

"I was freezing." She laughed, and her teeth chattered. She didn't think she would ever feel warm again.

"I couldn't tell. You were great. Maybe you could model for me sometime." He lowered his voice as he towered over her. In her heeled boots, he still stood a good two inches taller.

Madison's pulse raced faster than it had moments before in front of the camera. "That will never happen." She forced herself to look up at him.

"There you go saying *never* again." He grinned.

"That was great!" Nathan complimented as he reached them. "You helped us out of a tight spot today." He gave her a big hug. "As promised." He handed her a bag full of the samples she'd modeled. "Enjoy."

"Thank you. Those shoes are incredible." Madison shivered again.

Cole rubbed her arms. "We should get you back to the *Hummer*. You are freezing."

"Yes please, go on ahead." Nathan tossed Cole the keys to the vehicle. "We are about to wrap it up for today. I'll be with you two in a few moments."

Madison didn't pull away when Cole wrapped an arm around her shoulder and led her through the park toward the *Hummer*. *It's just for warmth*.

"You know, it did look like you were having fun, once your nervousness subsided." Cole helped her back into the *Hummer* and turned on the heater and seat warmer.

"I did." Madison placed her hands in front of the blast of hot air coming from the vents. "I hope Damian doesn't find out. *Do not* tell him." She pointed a finger at him.

"My lips are sealed, but it will cost you." His eyes gleamed with mischief.

Madison's narrowed.

"Fine, I won't tell him." Cole said with a laugh.

Nathan opened the driver side door and climbed into the *Hummer*. "But we have those *Giants* tickets for tonight's game." His cell phone rested on one shoulder. "No—of course, you're right—I'll be there." He shut the phone and sighed. He turned in his seat to face Madison. "Unfortunately there has been a slight change of plans for tonight. Becca's niece is singing in her school play, and she's forcing me to go." He faked a smile. "I won't be able to go to the football game tonight." He put the *Hummer* in reverse and backed out of the parking stall.

"That's too bad. I was looking forward to it." Cole pouted in the backseat. Madison shot him a look.

"But of course, family comes first."

"That doesn't mean you two can't go. The seats are incredible, someone should enjoy them." Nathan reached into his pocket and produced the tickets. He handed them to Cole.

"Oh no, we couldn't accept..." Madison stopped as Cole kicked the back of her seat.

"Shh...These are great seats, Madison."

"Really I don't mind." Nathan laughed. "We all make sacrifices in love, don't we?"

Madison could see many sacrifices in Nathan's future, but she bit her tongue. She hoped she was wrong and wished him and Becca a *lifetime* of happiness. Or six months, whichever came first. "Okay, if you're sure." Madison could see a big smile emerge on Cole's face through the side view mirror. She shook her head. *The man was a big child.*

"I am." Nathan pulled the *Hummer* in front of the hotel.

"It was a pleasure getting to know you," Madison said.

Cole opened the passenger side door and helped her climb down from the vehicle.

"The pleasure was mine." Nathan waved. "Merry Christmas. I'll be looking forward to reading the article."

Madison and Cole said *goodbye* to bachelor number two and headed inside the hotel.

"So, I'll meet you back here in the lobby at six thirty?" Cole hit the button for the elevator. He waved the football tickets in the air.

"You know, I think I'll pass on the game. All I want is a hot bath." It *wasn't a lie*. The late night, early morning, and slight hangover had exhausted her. She also couldn't wait to call Samantha. Her friend would be shocked to hear what she'd done.

"I could skip the game for a hot bath." Cole shrugged and leaned against the wall inside the elevator.

Madison stabbed the button for the third floor and glared at him. "I meant *alone*."

"Look Madison, if you haven't figured it out yet, I am a persistent man, and if you don't agree to go to the game with me, I'll find another way to see you tonight." The elevator stopped on their floor. He held the doors open, blocking her escape.

She hesitated. He wasn't kidding. *How dangerous could a football game be?* If he was like most men, he wouldn't even acknowledge her once the game started. *Much better than any alternative plans.* She sighed and shot him an annoyed look. A bath would have to wait.

"Fine." Madison shoved past him out into the hallway. "But just the game, then straight back here to the hotel. I mean it, Cole." She pointed a finger at him.

"Can't wait to get me back to the hotel huh?" He paused outside her room door.

"Cole." She shoved the key card into the lock.

"Okay, I promise. Just the game, nothing more." He gave her a *Scout's honor* sign.

Madison rolled her eyes and pushed her hotel room door open. She doubted he'd ever been a boy scout.

* * * *

Two hours later, Madison and Cole arrived at *Metlife Stadium* among a sell out crowd. The *Giants* were playing the *Kansas City Chiefs,* and the rivalry was intense.

"Have you ever been to an NFL game before?" Cole handed their tickets to a woman sporting a *New York Giant's* jersey behind a thin glass panel.

"No." Madison shook her head.

"You're in for a treat." Cole took her hand and led her through the large crowd of people to their sideline seats.

Madison wiggled her hand free once they'd reached their seats and sat as far away from him as possible in the cold plastic chair.

Cole looked away and smiled. *The woman was terrified of her feelings for him.* The walls protecting her heart were coming down, but it was a slow process. He was patient. Little by little he would break through as she learned to trust him. The details about her divorce were vague. One thing he knew for sure, the guy was an idiot for hurting her and letting her go. Once she was in his arms, he wouldn't be making *that* mistake. The intensity of his feelings for her normally would have sent him running. He hadn't allowed himself to fall this hard for a woman in years, but this was different. She was different, *special*. He had to convince her to give him a chance.

By halftime, Madison's voice was hoarse, and her cheeks were flushed with excitement.

"Can I get you a drink?" Cole asked.

"Yes, please. Wow. I didn't realize how exciting a live football game could be." She laughed. "My voice sounds terrible. Great first impression for bachelor number three in the morning."

"I'm glad you're enjoying yourself." He stood. "Be right back."

He returned a few moments later with their drinks and took his seat next to her as the Cheerleaders started their halftime routine, wearing cute Santa suits, and performing to the music of *Jingle Bell Rock*. Contrary to the eyes of every other man in the stadium, Cole couldn't take his eyes off of Madison.

"What?" Madison took a sip of her cold beer and toyed with the plastic lid of the cup. "The cheerleaders are that way." She gave a nervous laugh.

"I was thinking about how incredibly beautiful *you* are. And how your eyes light up when you let your guard down long enough to enjoy life." He stared at her hands and fought the urge to reach out to touch them. He didn't want to chance ruining the evening they were having by being too forward. Scott's advice rang in his mind. "Sometimes it's like you try hard not to let anyone see the real you, and it's a shame because you are wonderful."

Madison swallowed "I'm…careful," she said after a moment.

A commotion behind them caught their attention. The *Giant's* mascot approached their section, throwing t-shirts out into the stands.

"Hey over here!" Cole stood in the stands to get the mascot's attention.

The mascot turned and threw a t-shirt their way.

Cole caught it in one hand and handed it to Madison. "A souvenir from your first football game."

She unfolded the shirt and held it against her body. The fabric reached her knees. She laughed.

"Okay, so you can use it for a nightgown." Cole took a sip of his beer.

"Hey you two. Look up at the screen," a kid sitting behind Cole said.

Madison looked and gasped at her smiling face on the big screen. The smile faded. "What is that? Why are we on the screen?" Panic crept into her voice.

Cole's smile spread from ear to ear. *Finally another opportunity to kiss her.* This was perfect. *How could she blame this one on him?* "Well little lady, it looks like I'll be getting that kiss after all." He turned in his seat to face her, setting his beer on the floor next to his feet.

"Cole, no." Madison held up her hands and backed away.

The crowd chanted, "Kiss, kiss, kiss!"

"Sorry Madison. This is beyond my control." His mischievous grin reached his blue eyes as he leaned toward her.

"Come on, you two. Kiss already," the little boy behind them urged.

"What do you say, Madison? Can we give the fans what they want?" Cole reached forward and cupped her face between his strong hands, closing the gap between them until his lips were inches from hers.

"Oops." Cole heard the boy gasp before he felt the first drop of soda hit the top of his head. He jumped back as the little boy's soda spilled down the front of his shirt. *Dammit!* He grabbed for a napkin.

Madison laughed and handed him her napkin. "Can you admit now, this kiss is not meant to be?" She sat back in her seat and watched him clean up the liquid.

Forget that. Meant to be or not, he was getting that kiss. "Don't be so sure about that." He grabbed her and drew her toward him. He placed her arms around his neck, and his hands gripped her ribs. Before she could escape his grasp, his lips met hers. The kiss was forceful, deep, full of longing, and he didn't release her until he heard the satisfactory moan escape her pretty lips. *Better, much better.*

Chapter Six

A cool New York breeze rustled the last of the fall leaves beneath her feet as Madison returned from the corner café a few blocks from the hotel the following morning. Last night's beer and late night hadn't been the best idea. The coffee in the hotel room wasn't strong enough. Bachelor number three spent his holiday seasons on the ski slopes in Whistler, British Columbia, and Madison dreaded the trip. Their flight was at nine o'clock, and she was meeting Cole in the hotel lobby at seven to drive to the airport. She hadn't slept a wink. Replaying their kiss over and over behind her closed lids, she'd tossed and turned. The kiss had been unexpected, and she'd been defenseless to prevent it. It had been so long since a man had made her feel the way Cole did with a simple look. His touch stirred a longing in her she'd forgotten existed and his kiss… She couldn't let that happen again. One broken heart in her lifetime was more than enough. Cole Harris was sexy, kind, talented, but trouble. *Lots of trouble.* She groaned. She couldn't afford any more trouble, despite how bad she might crave it.

Cole loaded the truck in the hotel parking lot when she arrived back at the hotel.

"Good morning." She offered him an eggnog latte. A peace offering to soften the blow before telling him the kiss couldn't happen again. She rehearsed her speech in her head again—co-workers, professional, not interested, blah blah blah—*All lies.*

"No thanks." He shook his head and ignored the drink.

"Okay." She frowned, puzzled by his mood. She looked at the cup in her hand, wondering what to do with the disgusting thing. She sure as hell wouldn't drink it.

He tossed another suitcase in the back of the truck.

"Cole, about that kiss last night…" She shifted from one foot to the other, studying the ground.

"It shouldn't have happened. We are co-workers, and you are not interested in changing the status of that relationship. Did I get it all?" He stopped working and turned to face her, his hands on his waist.

She stood open-mouthed near the passenger side of the truck. The words stuck in her throat. *That* was *what she'd been planning to say, but...*

He glanced at his watch. "We are going to be late for the flight. Get in." He climbed into the driver's seat and slammed the door.

She looked around and spotted a garbage can near the hotel door. She jogged to it and tossed in the latte. *What was wrong with him?* Puzzled, disappointed and relieved, she climbed into the truck. *At least she wouldn't have to say it.*

This time of year, they were lucky to be on the same flight heading to Whistler. Therefore, they sat three rows apart in first class. Madison slid her laptop case under the seat in front of her and shot a glance in Cole's direction.

He didn't appear to be missing her. He laughed and flirted with the tall blonde occupying the seat next to him.

Madison fought the surge of jealousy rising. *What did she care anyway?* She didn't want a relationship with him. Her stomach turned, and she shifted in her seat. She had to quit lying to herself.

The girl giggled at something Cole said, and he wrapped his arm across the back of her seat to face her, ignoring the view from the window seat he'd insisted on. *So much for his motion sickness.* The girl glanced in her direction, and Madison swung around.

Battling another headache, she shrank lower in her seat and closed her eyes. *The blonde could have him, she didn't care.* The plane left the runway, and the next thing she heard was Cole's voice.

"Hey, wake up. We're here." He tapped her on the shoulder as he passed in the aisle.

Madison blinked the sleep from her eyes and gathered her things.

Cole didn't wait for her as she struggled to remove her carry on from the overhead compartment and pull her laptop from under the seat in front of her. She shot him an annoyed look, which he ignored.

She ran to catch up with him once inside the *Vancouver International Airport*. "Hey, what is the hurry?" She wiped her tired eyes. The three-hour nap hadn't been long enough. Groggy, she smoothed her dishevelled hair.

"We still have a two hour drive ahead of us up the mountain— that's if the driving conditions are good. This time of year, the weather is unpredictable, and it's snowing." Cole handed the company credit card to the car rental clerk.

"You've been here before? To Whistler?" He hadn't mentioned it.

"Yes, actually Madison, I meant to tell you before. Blake Ford is an old friend of mine." Cole picked up his luggage and headed toward the parking lot, keys in hand.

Bachelor number three, Blake Ford was a successful, Olympic snowboarder. *How did Cole know him?*

"Wait a second, do you know anymore of the remaining bachelors?" Madison stopped, and her heart raced. *Did he know Kurt too?*

"No, just Scott and Blake. It's one of the reasons I was offered the assignment." Cole tossed their luggage into the trunk of the car and slammed it shut.

His sulking was annoying. "What's gotten you in a rotten mood today?" She asked, slamming the passenger door shut. Last night they'd been laughing and getting along—and kissing. Now he appeared annoyed to be around her.

"Nothing." Cole started the car and turned on the windshield wipers. Heavy snow hit the window at an angle.

"Fine." Madison snapped her seatbelt and turned on the radio. Silence would be awkward. The sound of Christmas music filled the space between them, and Madison hummed *Silent Night* as she kicked off her boots and tucked her feet beneath her in the seat. She reached into her bag and pulled out a book. *Might as well get comfortable.*

Cole reached forward and switched the radio off. He took the book from her and tossed it into the back seat.

Madison shot him a puzzled look and glanced back at her book. "Hey!" *What was wrong with him?*

"Actually, Madison, it's not *nothing*." He turned to look at her. "Why didn't you tell me Kurt Davidson is your ex-husband?"

"How did you...?" Madison's mouth gaped. *Who told him? How long had he known?*

"I googled him last night at the hotel."

"I didn't mention it because, it doesn't matter." Madison's tone was cool and unfrazzled, but she fought to control her shaking hands. *So much for getting through the assignment without him knowing.*

"Doesn't matter? Did Damian know this before he gave you this assignment?" Cole frowned. He turned the wipers on higher and turned on the defogger to melt the snow on the windshield.

"No." Madison looked out the window. *Drop it, please.* The last person she wanted to discuss this with was Cole. Her ex-husband's affair had been a newsworthy event or at least the *Journal* had thought so, and she'd had to deal with the embarrassment and questions from everyone from family to strangers when the news broke. She'd put all of it behind her—sort of.

"Why didn't you tell him? Why did you accept the assignment?" Cole turned the car onto the Sea to Sky highway, heading north toward Whistler.

"Because I am a professional journalist, and this assignment will further my career." She'd repeated those words to herself many times over the course of the week.

"That's ridiculous..."Cole took his eyes off the road.

"Cole, watch out!" She put an arm up to shield her face as the car swerved to avoid hitting a deer dashing across the icy highway.

The car spiralled on the black ice and ended tail up in the ditch on the opposite side of the highway. A transport truck hit his horn as he narrowly avoided hitting them.

Madison's head bounced on the dash as the airbag failed to deploy.

Cole swung open the driver's side door and jumped out of the car. He climbed over the hood of the vehicle. "Madison, are you all right?" He opened her door and reached in. He unbuttoned her seatbelt and lifted her out of the car, ignoring her struggles and protests.

"I'm fine." She wiggled in his arms until he set her on the ground.

His trembling hands rested on her shoulders, a look of concern on his handsome face.

A huge bump formed on Madison's forehead. "Ouch!" She touched the purple, tender spot. Her eyes blurred, and she swayed in his arms.

Cole gripped her tight to steady her. "Maybe we should call an ambulance." He pushed her hair away from her face to get a better look at the injury.

"No really, I'm fine. Let's worry about getting this car out of the ditch and back onto the road." Madison shivered more from the impact of the crash, than the cold wind. Wet snow covered her jacket and clung to her hair.

Cars slowed as they passed them on the winding road, but no one stopped.

"Are you sure…?" Cole hesitated, his ice blue eyes filled with worry.

"I'm sure. Let's flag someone down to help us get back on the road." Madison's head throbbed, and she fought a wave of nausea. She removed his hands from her face and turned her attention to the traffic.

Minutes later a large four-wheel drive pulled over to the shoulder, and in no time they were back in the car on the road.

They drove in silence for what seemed an eternity.

"I'm sorry Madison." Cole didn't take his eyes from the road.

The speedometer hadn't gone above fifty since they'd resumed driving.

Madison glanced at him.

He didn't meet her gaze. His hand trembled on the gearshift.

She resisted the urge to touch him. "I'm fine. The accident wasn't your fault." Neither was her divorce or broken heart.

* * * *

Blake Ford was notorious for being an adventure seeking, risk taker linked to more than one rocky relationship with female celebrities. Three-time gold medal winner in the Winter Olympic snowboarding events and owner of a chain of snowboarding shops, Blake was a success on and off of the slopes. Madison doubted his Christmas traditions would be relaxing or low-key. Christmas tree decorating and hospital visits to sick children were not on the agenda with this bachelor.

Buzzing his Penthouse condo three hours later, she wasn't surprised he was still in bed. He opened the door in a pair of reindeer printed boxer shorts and nothing else.

"Hi...um...I'm Madison Grey." Madison's cheeks flushed. *Didn't anyone put a shirt on before answering a door?*

Blake blinked and ran a hand through his dishevelled, shoulder length blond hair. He gave her a confused look.

"From *Women's World Quarterly*."

"Okay...?" Blake still looked puzzled.

Oh no. He had no idea who she was or why she was here. *Typical Ashley.* The young receptionist couldn't be trusted with anything. She would have a long chat with her when she got back to Staten Island. First, giving out her address to a stranger, then dropping the ball on the assignment.

"Blake, man, go put on a shirt!" Cole appeared in the doorway behind an open mouthed Madison.

"Hey Cole! What are you...?" Realization dawned on Blake's face. He turned to Madison. "Madison—from the women's magazine." He pointed to her and snapped his fingers. "I'd totally forgotten that interview was this week. Wow, is it the twelfth of December already?" Blake laughed.

"Yes." Madison pursed her lips. *Sorry Ashley.*

Blake moved away from the door. "Come in, please. I'll get dressed and be right with you. Cole, help yourself. You know where I keep everything in the kitchen." Blake disappeared down the hall.

Cole shook his head and grinned. "The guy can't even put on some clothes to answer the door."

Madison hadn't been complaining about the view. Blake Ford was an ex-marine and his chest and bulging biceps indicated he kept himself in perfect shape. At least she couldn't complain about a shortage of attractive men on this assignment. She may not be interested in a relationship, but they were still easy on the eyes.

"Thanks." Madison removed her coat and walked around the spacious living room. Blake's winter home, where he spent the majority of his time had a fantastic view of the mountains. She stopped to gaze out a window.

"I didn't do it for you, I did it for me. He was making me look bad." Cole flashed her his famous grin.

She hadn't realized she'd missed it until now. The rest of the way to Whistler, they'd driven in silence as Cole concentrated on the winding roads. Conversation had been brief and superficial. Madison suspected he wanted to finish their discussion about her ex-husband and why she'd agreed to the assignment, but he didn't ask again. The conversation was bound to resurface, but she was happy to prolong the inevitable.

Blake emerged from his bedroom wearing a dark navy blue sweater and dark brown ski pants. If possible, he looked better dressed than he had half naked. His long, blond hair was tied at the base of his neck and the rough stubble on his chin was a testament to his easy-going, carefree lifestyle.

A tall, thin girl followed him into the living room. Dressed in what could only be described as a sweater stretched down over her hips and six-inch boots that reached above the knee the girl smiled and waved to Madison and Cole. "Hi." She giggled.

"Hi," Madison said.

Cole stood open mouthed.

Madison slapped his arm.

"Oh, yeah, hi." He fumbled with his camera bag.

Blake turned to the girl and wrapped an arm around her waist. He lowered his head to her neck.

The girl giggled and pushed him away. "Call me." She stood on tiptoes and kissed Blake's cheek.

"You got it." Blake winked and opened the door, ushering her out into the hallway. He turned his attention to Madison and Cole. "Sorry about that. I would have introduced you but for the life of me I couldn't remember her name...*Kimber? Tammy?*" He frowned. "Nope, can't remember."

"Would it be *Holly* by any chance?" Madison narrowed her eyes to a blue pen mark on his hand.

"That's it!" Blake's eyes widened, and he nodded. "How'd you know?"

Madison grabbed his hand and held it up for him to read the scribbled name and phone number. The ink was already too blurred to pick out the last three digits. *Guess Holly won't be getting a call.*

"Oh." Blake laughed and blushed. "Sorry—if I'd known—or *remembered* you were going to be here today…"

Madison shook her head. "No problem at all." *Now, how to gently describe this for the article?*

Blake turned to Cole. "Hey buddy! Long time." The two exchanged a handshake and pat on the back.

"Too long. What's on the agenda today?"

"Are you kidding?" Blake feigned a look of shock. "There's fresh powder on the slopes man. We are going skiing." He grinned and clapped his hands together.

Madison's eyes widened. *Skiing?* She hadn't skied in years. "I didn't bring any ski clothes." She'd hoped to avoid the sport. "I'll watch you two ski." *Definitely the safer option.* She already had one injury so far on this leg of the trip. She didn't want to add any broken bones to it.

"No way. These mountains are amazing." Blake shook his head at her protests. "Up the stairs, the second door on the right." Blake pointed upstairs. "In the guest room closet you will find everything you need."

Madison sighed and headed up the stairs. If she'd learned one thing so far on this assignment, it was that no one was taking her "no" for an answer.

* * * *

The ski slopes were warmer than Madison had expected, but she was grateful for the cashmere sweater she wore under her ski jacket. Her second attempt to convince the men she would prefer to watch them ski and not don a pair of skis herself had failed. Standing at the top of a ski run labeled *In deep*, she smiled at the irony. Her legs shook, and the hill looked bigger from the top. Staring down the icy hill, Madison forced herself once again to remember why she'd taken this assignment in the first place. Broken bones were *not* on her Christmas list. She was asking for a raise in the New Year if assignments like this were added to her job description.

"Race you to the bottom." Cole appeared next to her on the hill.

"It wouldn't even be a challenge. I can barely stand on these skis." She laughed and held up her ski poles.

"I'd gladly fall behind to watch your sexy ass in those ski pants." He winked as he took off down the hill.

Her face flushed as she watched him make his way down the slope, his hips moving back and forth with expertise. He made it look easy. Maybe she should remove the skis and walk down the hill. While that would be embarrassing, so would wiping out. She weighed her options. Either way she couldn't keep standing there. A group of school aged students on a field trip whizzed by her.

"What are you waiting for? Do you want me to come get you?" Cole called from the bottom of the hill.

Not a chance. That was the motivation she needed. She pushed off and started down the hill. She moved as slow as she could and with caution. *Okay, this isn't so bad. Almost there.* She let out a breath she'd been holding as she neared the bottom.

"See, that wasn't so bad." Cole held out an arm as she approached him at the base of the hill. An amused smile spread across his handsome features. Behind his sunglasses his eyes glinted.

She caught his arm and rotated as her skis slowed to a stop. "Whoa." She stumbled and struggled to balance. "Thanks." She let go off his arm and moved out of the way as the school kids ran past on their way to the chair lift.

"Going back up?" Cole pushed off and headed in the direction of the lift.

"Ah, I don't know…" Madison glanced up the hill. It hadn't been *that* bad. Maybe after a few more runs, she'd get the hang of it.

Blake shot down the hill and stopped inches from them. "Having fun yet?" His face was flushed with exhilaration.

Cole nodded. "Madison's a little nervous."

She blushed and shot him a look. "I haven't been skiing in years." She shrugged.

"No problem. Come on, I'll teach you a few basic moves on the Bunny slope, and in less than an hour you'll be skiing like the pros." Blake took her arm.

"I doubt that, but okay." Madison gave Blake a smile. She turned and stuck her tongue out at Cole as the two skied away.

He looked disappointed. She'd abandoned him so easily for lessons from his playboy friend.

At the t-bar lift, Blake held it steady as she climbed onto one side. He glanced toward the chair lift and laughed.

"What?" Madison turned to see Cole sandwiched between two young girls on the chair as it made its way to the top of the hill. He looked uncomfortable.

Blake shook his head. "I'll never understand that guy." He chuckled as the t-bar started with a jolt.

Madison tore her eyes away from Cole. "What do you mean?"

"You know, he's hot…"

"He's okay." Madison blushed. *Yes he was, but discussing that with Blake might be blurring the professional line a little.*

"Okay, maybe *you* don't think so…" Blake pinched her crimson cheek. "But ninety-nine percent of the women out there do, and yet, the man never gets laid."

Madison lost her grip on the handle and fought to regain her balance. She hadn't been expecting *that.* Talk about crossing the professionalism line. At this point, she knew too much about him already. She wasn't sure how much more she wanted to hear. She coughed.

"Sorry, forgot I was talking to a chick." Blake laughed.

Chick?

"Let me put it another way, he doesn't date—ever." He shrugged. "Makes no sense to me."

"That is strange." Madison frowned. Her curiosity peaked. "So, you two have been friends for a long time?" The pair didn't seem likely.

"Since college. We were roommates." Blake helped her off of the metal bar at the top of the learner's slope. Children and a few awkward adults littered the hill. "He had a girlfriend then, but since they broke up in junior year, he's only dated a handful of women, and only once or twice."

That part wasn't surprising. He was a player. Just as she'd thought. He'd himself admitted he wasn't the marrying type.

"I always thought he was upset when she called off the engagement, but I think it's long overdue to get over it." Blake shrugged. "Okay, stand with your feet shoulder width apart." He grabbed her shoulders and positioned her on the hill.

Engagement? He'd been engaged?

"Earth to Madison." Blake waved a hand in front of her dazed look.

"Oh sorry, what were you saying?"

Blake stood back and studied her. He folded his arms across his chest and glanced at her above his sunglasses. "Do you want to learn to ski or do you want to learn more about the photographer you think is *okay?*"

Madison looked toward the ski slope where Cole dashed down the hill with ease. So, he'd been hurt. That would explain the aversion to marriage. According to Blake, he wasn't the playboy she'd pegged him to be either. Skiing was definitely the safer option.

* * * *

Cole paced the ski lodge foyer a few hours later. The heat radiating from the big stone fireplace made him sweat in his crew neck sweater and leather jacket. He wiped his sweaty palms on his jeans and checked his watch. Madison was three minutes late. *Please don't let her reconsider*. Her acceptance of his dinner proposal had surprised him, and he hoped she wouldn't change her mind. He smiled remembering the look of fear on her face at the top of the ski hill earlier that day. He had to give her credit though, she was brave. She'd impressed the hell out of him on the snowmobile, racing both him and Blake to the lake *and* back. *Evidently, she liked speed...at least in motorized vehicles*. He suspected she was far more cautious with her heart.

The sound of heels on the wooden staircase made him turn. He smiled at the sight of her descending the stairs. Dressed in a black pencil skirt and knee-high boots, she looked incredible. His breath caught in his throat as he gave a small wave.

She cradled her cell phone against her shoulder as she slid her purse over her arm. She smiled and waved as she approached. "Okay, I have to go. I'll call you as soon as I get back to Staten Island." *Sorry,* she mouthed to him.

No problem, he mouthed back.

"Okay, bye. Love you too."

Cole's heart stopped. *Love you too. Who was she talking to?* His eyes lowered to the floor, and he fought the urge to ask as she hung up the phone.

"Sorry. My mom." She rolled her eyes. "It's near impossible to get her off of the phone."

Relief flowed through him. *Her mother. Thank God.* He didn't want to have to steal her from some other guy. But if he had to, he would. *That* he knew for sure. "No problem." He gestured toward the door. "It stopped snowing, and the restaurant is a few blocks, do you mind if we walk?"

Madison shook her head. "Not at all."

"Great." Cole smiled and held the door for her.

"Wow, it is beautiful here in the mountains. Do you spend much time here?" Madison slid her hands into her leather gloves as they descended the steps of the lodge.

"During the four years in college, we spent every Christmas break here, but since graduating I've only been here a couple of times. Only when Blake is competing." Cole shrugged. He turned to her with a gleam in his eye. "So, what do you think of our Bachelor number three?"

Madison grinned and studied the icy sidewalk beneath her feet. "He's interesting. Definitely different from the first two."

Cole laughed. "That's for sure. He is a great guy though. His grandparents raised him after his parents died in an avalanche when he was a child. They were hiking, here in Whistler." Cole lowered his voice.

"Really?" Madison frowned. "That's awful. I'm surprised Blake doesn't have an aversion to this place because of that." She shivered.

"Yeah, it's strange, but he said when he's here on the slopes he feels closer to them."

"I guess I can understand that." Madison nodded.

Cole stopped. "Here we are." He held open the front door to the restaurant and stood back to let her go inside ahead of him. The *Edgewater Lodge* was located on the outskirts of Whistler Village next to a beautiful frozen lake. Decorated in white lights and candles, the atmosphere was rated one of the most romantic places to dine in Canada. There was something magical about a restaurant at the top of a beautiful mountain, miles away from everyday life.

"How did you know about this place?" Madison asked as a waiter guided them to a secluded booth near a window.

"Thank you." Cole nodded to the waiter as he pulled out a chair for Madison. "I asked some of the locals where I could find a nice place to take a special lady." Cole smiled. His source of information was Blake, who was busy teaching nighttime snowboarding lessons to teens. Despite his playboy image, Blake had a heart of gold. He spent most of his spare time volunteering at the lodge, offering free skiing and snowboarding lessons to tourists.

The waiter reappeared with a bottle of red wine. "Compliments of Blake Ford." He set the bottle down and left.

"That was nice of him." Madison said.

"He's a great guy. Wine?" Cole poured her a glass, not waiting for a response. "It was a rhetorical question." He laughed. He'd just assumed her answer.

"Thank you." She sipped her red wine.

Cole stared at her hands on the glass. *Small and slender, yet strong and soft. An irresistible combination.* He reached forward to touch one. She stiffened at the contact, but didn't pull away. *Good sign.*

"Tell me more about your family. Are they still in California?" He leaned forward, resting his elbows on the table.

"My parents are." She nodded. "My father is a human rights lawyer and my mom never worked outside of the home after my brother and I were born. She insisted on staying home with us, and Dad agreed it was the way it should be. They've been married for almost forty years." Madison toyed with the stem of her wine glass with her free hand.

"And you have one brother?" Cole traced a finger along her thumb, daring to tighten his grip on her hand.

"Yes, Jake. He lives in Europe with his wife Melanie and their two young boys. Colin is six and Marcus is four. I don't see them often, but we keep in touch." Madison said. "And you? Any other siblings?"

"Nope, just Mel and I, our mom raised us on her own. She lives in a senior's home in Florida, and I fly down to visit every few months." He shrugged and looked sheepish. "I was supposed to be there this week."

"You canceled a visit with your mom for this assignment?" Madison clucked her tongue. "You should be ashamed of yourself."

"I'm sure if she met my travel companion, she would understand. Besides, I plan to spend a few weeks in Florida in the New Year with her. Right now, traveling with a beautiful woman from one winter wonderland to the other sounds like the perfect holiday season to me." Cole stared into her eyes. *Man, she was beautiful*. He resisted the urge to tell her. *Take it slow with this one*. It was difficult when her pretty lips beckoned to be kissed. "So, do you enjoy working at *Women's World*?" He took a sip of wine and studied her.

She lowered her eyes to the table and took a minute to respond. "Um—yes and no."

"How so?"

"I love the industry and editing used to be a passion of mine…"

"But…"

"Now I'm ready for more challenges. Writing assignments mostly." She pushed a stray lock of hair behind her ear.

"That's why you accepted this less than ideal assignment?" *That would explain it. Why else would she have agreed to interview her ex-husband for an article on New York's most eligible bachelors?* He admired her ambition. This couldn't be easy for her. No wonder she hadn't been exciting about this whole thing.

"I guess." She nodded. "I've been asking Damian for a writing assignment for months, so when the opportunity presented itself…" She shrugged one shoulder.

"You couldn't refuse."

She nodded.

The waiter approached their table and announced the evening's special of roasted chicken and seasonal vegetables, which they both ordered. He collected their menus, refilled their water glasses and left.

"Your real passion is writing?" He remembered the few paragraphs he'd read on her laptop a few days before.

"Yes." Her eyes came alive at the mention of it. They met his. "I recently finished a novel." She glanced through the window.

"Seriously?" *A novel? That was impressive.* He could barely write a letter. His creative ability ended at photography.

She nodded.

"That's fantastic. Have you submitted it to a publisher?"

"Yes, and waiting for a reply is torture." She laughed, and her shoulder's relaxed. She sipped her wine and licked the liquid from the rim of the glass.

Cole leaned toward her and lowered his voice. "No, torture is sitting this far away from you." *So much for not being forward.* He paused, waiting for her reaction.

She smiled and cocked her head to the side. "There's room on this side for both of us." Her voice was low as she moved in further on her side of the booth, leaving enough room for him to join her.

The gesture surprised him, but he was up in a flash. He slid in next to her and wrapped one arm around the back of the booth, turning to face her. "I know you said you wouldn't kiss me again, but I'm not sure I can let that happen." His face lowered, and he brushed a strand of hair away from her cheek.

Her eyes met his in the candlelight. "What are you waiting for?"

* * * *

The December sun shone through Madison's window the next morning, and she awoke feeling fresh and revived long before her alarm went off. This was their last day with bachelor number three, and she had to admit she was disappointed to leave this wonderful winter village. She stretched and tossed the covers aside. She opened a package of coffee and started the maker. Pulling back the curtains to the window, she sat on the window seat, drawing her legs up beneath her. Looking at the mountains she sighed.

The night before had been nothing short of magical. After dinner they'd taken a horse-drawn sleigh ride through the village, enjoying the festive sights and sounds. Cole had revealed more about his career ambitions and had been genuinely curious about her passion for writing. She could no longer deny the feelings developing for her colleague. He was nothing like she'd pegged him to be. When he'd walked her to her room the night before, his eyes had revealed his desire to continue the night inside her room, but he'd kissed her and said goodnight. It had taken most of her strength not to invite him inside, but she wasn't ready for that yet. For now, they were still co-workers first and foremost. Maybe once they finished this assignment that could change. She smiled at the thought.

Her cell phone vibrated on the desk near the bed. She picked it up and smiled. *Samantha.* "Hello." Madison curled up on the bed and leaned back against the pillows.

"Hi Madison." Samantha said. "How are you?"

"Good. I tried calling your cell phone last night, but it said you were out of the calling area?" Madison examined her chipped toe polish. Maybe she would get a pedicure. She had time. Blake wouldn't be out of bed until at least one after a late night of partying.

"I wish." Samantha laughed. "No, Mason flushed my cell phone down the toilet last night. *I'm* still within the calling area, my phone isn't."

Poor Samantha. Madison shook her head. Her friend's hands were certainly full with those boys. "How's work?"

"I honestly don't know how you handle these acquisitions." She huffed.

"Oh no. Damian is making you do them?" Madison cringed. She doubted Samantha had as much sympathy for the hopeful writers, and she hoped she wasn't crushing too many dreams.

"Yes, hurry back."

"Have you found any decent submissions at least?" Maybe her friend would experience better luck than she had.

"What do you think?" Her friend gave a dry laugh.

"That bad?" Madison took her compact and tweezers from her purse. She cradled the phone against her shoulder and plucked a few stray hairs from her eyebrows.

"Worse. So, how are you?" Concern filled her tone.

"Good...great actually." Madison was unable to conceal her happiness.

"Really?" Samantha sounded hesitant to believe her.

She couldn't blame her friend for being skeptical. A week ago she'd been pegging this assignment as the worst thing that could ever have happened. Now, she was less pessimistic. She still dreaded the fact she would be seeing Kurt again for the first time in almost three years, but the rest of the assignment was going smoothly so far. She touched the bump on her forehead. *Okay, except for that.* "Yes, really." She recalled an image of the horse-drawn sleigh.

"What's with the change of heart? Ten days ago, I was afraid of leaving you alone for fear of finding you hanging from your shower rod."

"I know. Sorry about that." She hated worrying her friend. Samantha had enough to worry about with three rambunctious boys.

"What's changed?"

"At first this assignment felt like a train wreck, and Cole—he was something I didn't want to deal with, but now—I don't know, the mountains and the sights and sounds of Christmas..." Madison rambled. A smile spread across her face as she stretched her legs out in front of her on the bed.

"Oh my God. You're falling in love with Cole." Samantha said.

"No!" Madison shook her head. "No, I'm not." *Was she? No, of course not.* That would be ridiculous. She barely knew Cole.

"It's just the holiday season. You know, all the Christmas festivities." Madison shrugged and pulled a blanket over her bare legs.

"No it's not. You hate the season. Cole Harris is responsible for this change of mood. You are one hundred percent head over heels for the man." Her friend's tone left no room for argument.

Madison sighed. "I'm not *in love*…I just like him." It was futile to fight with Samantha, the one person who knew her better than she knew herself. She recounted the events of the previous evening.

"And after all that wining and dining, he *didn't* try to sleep with you?" Samantha sounded shocked.

Madison laughed. "Nope. He was a perfect gentleman. I mean I could tell he was dying to ask if he could come inside my room, but he resisted that natural male jerk-ish impulse."

"Well if you won't fall in love with him, step aside, I just might." Samantha laughed. "I am still jealous that you got this assignment. I mean, other than the ex-husband issue, it's a fantastic piece. Christmas festivities, traveling, gorgeous, successful men. Speaking of gorgeous, successful men, how was Nathan Harper?" Samantha's tone took on a dreamlike quality.

Madison laughed. "As perfect as you can imagine. He's better looking in person, and a great guy with humble beginnings." Madison couldn't wait to write about the men she'd met so far. Blake would be the biggest challenge, but she was learning, there was more to him than his playboy persona.

"I'm so jealous."

"I do have a surprise for you." Madison remembered, seeing the edge of the *Gucci* bag sticking out of her open suitcase.

"Please tell me its Nathan wrapped in a big bow."

"I'm not sure Mike would appreciate that." Madison smiled. Her friend was joking. Samantha wouldn't trade her husband for *any* man. Madison envied the love and commitment her friend had in her relationship. "But, it does have the *NH* initials embroidered on it."

"No way. Seriously? How did you…?"

"Don't ask. You owe me though." Samantha would never believe how she'd come to get her Christmas present. She shook her head and shivered at the memory.

"I think we're even. Do you know how hard your job is?"

"Fair enough." Madison laughed.

"Definitely hurry back. I want my present. Shit, my next appointment is here." Samantha lowered her voice. "Yes Sophie, tell her I'll be with her in a moment." She told her assistant. "I gotta go, call me again soon."

"Okay, but before you go, did I mention I'm staring at beautiful snow covered mountains from the window of a five star lodge?" She couldn't pass up the opportunity to tease her friend.

"I hate you." Samantha hissed and hung up.

Madison shut her cell phone and gazed out at the mountains. Of course she wasn't in love with Cole. She'd only known him a few weeks. Part of that time she hadn't even liked him. It was the season and the spirit of these wonderful snow covered mountains. She liked him and would like to spend more time with him…but love? Oh well, she'd know soon enough. The next day, they were headed to bachelor number four's family home in Tuscumbia, Alabama. How romantic could that be?

Chapter Seven

If Madison hoped to escape the spirit of Christmas by leaving her British Columbia winter wonderland, she'd gone to the wrong place. Arriving in the small town of Tuscumbia, Alabama the community welcome sign revealed they were entering *Plantation Christmas Country, population 1623*. Madison had done her research on the plane and had discovered each year, for the entire month of December, the whole community recreated an early 19th century holiday celebration in the town. Traditional entertainment from the era and decorations reflecting the *Old South* brought the community to life. Pictures on the town's own website showcased previous years' events. Avoiding Christmas was not a possibility in Tuscumbia.

Bachelor number four, Dr. Rod Livingston had been born and raised in Tuscumbia. Each year, he closed his medical practice in New York for two weeks and returned to his family home for the holidays.

"This should be interesting." Cole surveyed the town as they drove down *Main Street*.

"There is literally *no one* around." Madison shook her head in shock and laughed. At three o'clock in the morning in New York, the city was as busy and crowded as it was any time of day. She glanced at her watch. 4:47 in the afternoon, and the community was a ghost town. "Where is everyone?"

"My guess would be the annual tree lighting ceremony in the *Town Square*." Cole gestured to a sign on the side of the road. *Tree Lighting this way.* A big arrow pointed the way. "Should we head straight over there?"

Madison glanced at the town map they'd picked up at the airport. "The Livingston family home is a couple of blocks that way," She pointed down a side street. "Maybe we should go there first, just in case."

"Okay." Cole pulled the rental car onto the side street.

Madison gasped. "My God, look at these homes." Large three-story Plantation manors lined both sides of the street. The space between each was wide enough to squeeze multiple brownstones.

"Yeah, and I bet they cost a fraction of what your condo on Staten Island costs." He grinned. "Definitely one of the benefits of living in a small town these days."

"But it's so quiet." No taxis honked or police sirens wailing in the distance. People weren't fighting for space on the crosswalks. In fact, she didn't even see a crosswalk.

"So, I take it you are a big city girl." Cole laughed.

Madison grinned. "Afraid so. Staten Island is the right size for me. Any smaller would be too small."

Cole turned the car into the Livingston's driveway and shut off the engine. Two cars were parked in the driveway, but the blinds were closed, and no light shone through the front windows. "Doesn't look like anyone's here." He peered through the windshield.

"I think there's a note on the door." Madison opened the passenger door. "I'll go look."

At the door, a piece of paper flapped in the breeze. She pulled it from the door. *Cole, Madison, Welcome to Tuscumbia. We have gone to the tree lighting in the Town Square. Look for the man in the red suit, and you'll be sure to find me. Rod.*

That's nice. Rod must dress up as Santa for these local events. Madison folded the note and tucked it into her coat pocket. She jogged back to the car. "You were right, they are at the tree lighting. Rod must dress up as Santa." She showed Cole the note.

"Should we leave the car here and walk?" Cole climbed out of the car and flung his camera bag over his shoulder.

"Sure." Madison was enjoying their time alone together, and the idea of an extra few minutes warmed her.

As they started down the sidewalk, Cole reached out and took Madison's gloved hand. Heat from his bare hand seared through her thin gloves, and she didn't even consider pulling away. The action was natural, nice, comfortable.

"Your hands are warm." She moved closer to him to enjoy the heat he radiated. The weather forecast predicted temperatures below freezing in Tuscumbia for the duration of their stay, and the air was colder here than Whistler's milder climate.

"They always are." Cole stopped in front of her and placed both hands against her rosy, cold cheeks. "You are beautiful," he said. His gentle gaze was a new source of heat, and Madison warmed through to her core. The kindness and sincerity in his eyes were something she hadn't seen in a long time. *How had she been dreading spending the season with him?* At that moment there was nowhere she would rather be. Her eyes pleaded with him to kiss her, and she didn't have to wait long for his response.

He slid his hands from her face to encircle her tiny waist. He pulled her closer into the warmth between them and lowered his lips to hers.

Madison sighed. She could forget about getting relief from her romantic feelings in Tuscumbia.

As they rounded the corner onto *Main Street,* the *Town Square* came into view. The large crowd gathered in the town center was incredible. If the welcome sign's population number was correct, all 1623 residents were attending this Christmas tradition, plus two. From a distance they could see the Santa Village, set up to the right of the thirty-foot evergreen tree the town's residents decorated. The multi-colored lights had been added, and the children hung huge snowflakes and candy canes to the tree's large branches. Madison had never seen a community activity quite like it.

"That looks like our guy right over there." Cole gestured to the big man dressed as Santa sitting in a big chair in the middle of Santa's Village. A photographer poised ready to take his photo with a little girl who wasn't impressed by the whole situation. She wailed and struggled on Santa's lap until the photographer shrugged and snapped the unflattering photo anyway.

To the sound of groans and complaints from the children waiting their turn, Madison and Cole made their way to the front of the line. Cole waved to Santa. He motioned for them to approach.

"Hi Ro...Santa." Madison extended a hand to Santa. "I'm Madison Grey from *Women's World Quarterly,* and this is Cole Harris." Madison smiled.

"Oh yes, I remember Rod mentioning something about being interviewed for a Women's magazine. He said you two would arrive today. Nice to meet you both," the man said in a jolly deep voice.

"You're not..." Confusion clouded Madison's face. *Hadn't Rod's note said he was playing Santa at the festivities?*

"Of course not, I'm Kris Kringle." He gave a belly-shaking laugh and winked at the children in line. He motioned for the next one to approach. Lowering his voice he said, "Rod is over in the fenced pen area with the other reindeer. He's Prancer this year." He pointed to the fenced off area to the right of the Santa hut.

Madison and Cole turned. All eight of Santa's reindeer grazed in their own pen labeled with a gold nameplate. *Prancer* was in the middle. Cole laughed at the sight of the eight men dressed in brown reindeer suits and antlers, baying in the pen for the attention of the children onlookers.

"Cole, stop laughing." Madison scolded, collapsing in a fit of giggles. She buried her face in Cole's shoulder, and her body shook with laughter.

"Can't you picture a set up like this in *Rockefeller Center*?" Cole wrapped an arm around her.

Rod noticed them and waved them over with his left hoofed hand.

"Uh, I think we've been spotted."

Madison moved away and wiped the tears from her eyes. She struggled to compose herself as they made their way to the reindeer pens.

Rod disappeared through the back curtain on the pen and gestured for them to meet him on the other side.

"Madison, Cole, please give me a second to change out of costume, and I'll be right with you. Why don't you wait for me inside the café?" He smiled and gestured to the small bakery and café next to the ice rink.

Madison smiled and nodded, not trusting herself to speak. *Thank God, he was changing first*. She didn't think she could sit across from him dressed like that. Those leggings left nothing to the imagination.

Cole opened the door to the café, and the smell of homemade apple pie and cinnamon lattes filled the shop.

Madison's stomach growled.

"Hungry little lady?" Cole whispered, as his own stomach let out its own cry for food.

Madison laughed. "I hadn't realized I was until the smell of the homemade goods." She scanned the display case. Muffins, cakes, pies and cookies tempted her from behind the glass.

"Just take a seat anywhere folks. I'll be right with you." A short, petite, blonde waitress called to them from a table in the corner where she jotted an order on a pad of paper.

"Oh okay." Madison couldn't conceal her surprise. *The waitress was bringing them their order?*

She slid into a booth near the window, and Cole slid in next to her. He opened the menu on the table. "Two dollars for a slice of homemade apple pie?" His eyes widened. "In New York, they'd charge eight fifty."

Rod entered the café and slid into the booth opposite them. In jeans and a crew neck sweater, he looked more like the picture Madison had seen of him in the medical journal the month before. However, his demeanor was much more relaxed here in Tuscumbia.

"Have you two ordered yet?"

"Not yet, but at these prices, I think I'll have one of everything on the menu." Cole had yet to look up from the laminated, homemade menu.

Madison laughed.

"I know. Before I head back to the city in January, I always take a six-month supply of baked goods with me. It lasts me until my summer visit." Rod waved to the waitress. "Anita, when you're ready, could we get a round of apple pies and lattes over here for my fellow New Yorkers."

"Coming right up, Dr. Rod." The woman smiled and cut into an apple pie fresh from the oven.

"It's great to meet you, Dr. Livingston." Madison extended a hand across the table.

"Oh, please call me, Rod. It's great to meet you both. I'll admit I'm a little surprised that your magazine wanted to include me in this article. With my thinning hair and expanding mid section, I don't see myself as one of New York's most eligible bachelors." He shook his head and patted an imaginary stomach.

Madison shook her head. From where she sat, he was an incredible looking man at forty. He would capture the attention of many women upon entering a room. "Of course you are considered a top eligible bachelor—single, attractive and your charitable work for the city would melt any woman's heart."

He blushed. "Thank you. You are too kind. What do you think of Tuscumbia so far?"

An image of Rod in his reindeer suit flashed in her mind, and she repressed an urge to laugh. "This place looks wonderful. It's really something to see the whole community coming together like this."

"Yeah, it's really something." Cole nodded.

"It is the best place to celebrate the season." Pride for his hometown was evident in his voice. "The last four generations of the Livingston family have celebrated Christmas here in Tuscumbia. No matter where we are in the world, at Christmas time, we all come home."

"Here you are folks. Enjoy." Anita placed three of the biggest slices of pie Madison had ever seen on the table in front of them. The waitress winked at Rod and Madison noticed a slight sway of her hips as she walked back to the counter. No doubt for his benefit, and Rod enjoyed the show, his eyes never leaving her curvy hips.

Cole cleared his throat.

Rod gave an embarrassed laugh. "Sorry, there's a history between us."

One, Madison suspected he'd like to repeat. She picked up a fork and took a bite of her pie. *Delicious.* She licked the apple filling off of the edge of the fork.

"How have your travels been?" Rod asked.

"Better than I could have imagined." Cole grinned and brushed a hand across Madison's cheek to remove a stray lock of dark hair from her face.

Her face turned a shade of crimson, and she choked on her pie. Her heart raced as Cole squeezed her knee under the table.

"It's…going…good." She nodded. *He had to stop touching her when they were with the bachelors. His effect on her was too obvious.*

Rod looked from one to the other, taking in the scene before him.

"Good." He nodded as he took a mouthful of pie. "You two are a couple. That will make things easier." Rod took a big gulp of his cinnamon latte and sat back in the booth.

"Oh, we are not…" Madison shook her head. They hadn't gotten as far as discussing what they were. *Friends? Dating?*

"Easier for what?" Cole asked.

Madison's protests died on her lips. Cole's question was more important than her defense of their yet undefined relationship.

"I was hoping to wait before springing this on you two, because the McMillan family *could* be here any day, but as of right now we are missing a Bob Cratchet and his wife for the annual *Christmas Carol* play." Rod shovelled the last of his pie into his mouth. "We were hoping you two would be kind enough to fill in. There is no one else to ask."

Madison's mouth fell open. He wanted them to act in their Christmas play? "Oh no, I don't think…" Madison kicked Cole under the table for help with her protests.

He remained silent.

Tell me he isn't going to agree to this. She glanced at him and was relieved to see he looked as terrified as she was. "We can't. We are here to document *your* traditions…" Madison explained hastily.

"Nonsense, what better way to observe than to participate? Besides, you two are stuck here for three days anyhow." Rod shrugged. "And the play means so much to the kids. It would be a shame to cancel it." Rod gave a pathetic pleading look.

Oh no, seriously? Madison sighed. So far on this trip no one was paying any attention to her *no's*. First the Christmas decorating, the photo shoot, the skiing—she shivered at the memory. *How many people would they be making a fool of themselves in front of? 1623 minus the McMillan family.* "Okay, fine. We'll do it." She held her hands up.

Cole shot her a look of panic. "What?"

Madison smiled. "It'll be fun." She had done some acting in a local theater as a teenager. *Maybe this wouldn't be so bad, and it was for children.*

"That's the spirit." Rod nodded in approval.

"But I need to photograph the whole thing." Cole let out a sigh of relief. "I guess that means I won't be able to be in the play." He licked apple filling from the corner of his lip.

"You don't have to worry about that. We hire a local team to photograph and video the whole thing. The local high school students are doing it for extra credit." Rod smiled over the rim of his mug. "They can provide you with a copy of any you may want."

"Perfect." Madison gave Cole a smug look. *Let's see how* he *does out of* his *comfort zone.*

"Yeah, perfect." Cole mumbled, draining the contents in his cup.

Rod winked at Madison across the table.

She winked back. *This* should be fun.

* * * *

The rehearsal room, in the basement of the community church was a buzz of activity as parents and children practiced the lines of their scripts and got into their costumes for fittings. In one corner, a group of carollers practiced their songs, and Madison smiled at the familiar sounds. *A Christmas Carol* was one of her favorite Christmas movies. She loved the original version, and her family had watched it every Christmas Eve. Madison knew almost every line by memory.

"Wow, I can't believe how many people are here." She surveyed the room. *Would there be anyone left to watch the production?*

"I play the same part every year," a man to the right of Madison said. He stood with his arms out at his sides. A seamstress added pins to his jacket.

"And he has to get the costume let out every year too," the seamstress teased with a mouthful of pins.

"*That* is true I'm afraid." The man laughed.

"We are looking for the costume room. Can you point us in the right direction?" Madison smiled at the older man.

"Down the hall, third door on the right." He nodded in the direction.

"Thank you."

"I still cannot believe we are doing this." Cole dragged his feet as they made their way to the costume room for their fitting. "Why on earth did you give in?"

"What choice did I have?" Madison said, but she smiled at the sight of children dancing in the hallway. She shrugged. "Besides it might be fun." This sudden wholehearted acceptance of the Christmas season was a shock to her, but this assignment kept making it impossible to remain a Grinch.

"I think I liked you better when you hated Christmas." Cole opened the door and entered the costume room.

Madison chuckled. "Sorry." She gave a sheepish look. "I guess it's true what they say. If you can't beat 'em, join 'em."

"There you two are, welcome! The couple I've been waiting for." Rod Livingston's mother, Evelyn, greeted them as they entered the room.

"You must be Evelyn. Great to meet you." Madison said.

Cole shied away in the corner. She'd never seen him this way. She grinned. "Don't pay no mind to Scrooge, he's just upset he doesn't get to play the lead." Madison teased, and Evelyn chuckled.

"Bob Cratchet and his wife are my favorite characters." Evelyn pulled Cole into the room. "Now let's get you fitted." She placed her hands on her hips and waited for Cole to remove his coat.

Reluctantly he obliged and slid into the Bob Cratchet costume.

"Wonderful fit." Evelyn clapped her hands. "I won't have to do much work with it at all." She grabbed a few pins from her sewing tray.

Madison gave Cole a *thumbs up* sign.

His eyes narrowed, and he shook his head. He mouthed the words, *I am only doing this for you.*

Madison smiled. *I know.*

* * * *

"Can I help you with anything?" Madison poked her head into the kitchen of the Livingston's home a few hours later. The mouth-watering scent of a baked ham and potatoes cooking in the oven made her stomach growl.

"No thanks dear. Everything's under control. Once my daughter Natalie and her husband Nick arrive, we can eat." Evelyn smiled and waved her away.

"Okay. Would you mind if I explored your house?" She'd been dying to see the rest of the home since they arrived.

"Not at all. Feel free to wander." She mixed a few ingredients in a bowl and turned on the hand mixer.

"Thanks." Madison let the swinging door close behind her and ventured out into the hall.

The old home carried an essence of the community itself. Old fashioned in a traditional, warm, inviting way. Built in the 1800's each room had its own fireplace. Each was decorated with fake snow and different Christmas themes. The dust accumulating on the ornaments suggested the Christmas decorating started early in the Livingston home. The original hardwood floor in the house had been re-stained in recent years to create a modern light and dark wood pattern and the warm colors of brown and blue paint on the walls enhanced the cozy, family atmosphere of the home.

Family pictures lined the hallways and Madison smiled, studying the school photos of Rod and his sister Natalie. He'd always had a playful, warm smile and gentle eyes. Maybe Evelyn would have a copy of his high school graduation photo for her article.

She descended the staircase and rejoined the men in the living room. Rod and his father Clyde were engaged in a chess match. Cole sat on an ottoman observing the game.

"Who's winning?" She placed her hands on her hips and glanced at the chessboard.

"I've never won a game, *ever*." Rod grinned at Madison as he moved a horse-shaped piece to the right, taking one of his father's smaller pieces.

"They've been playing this one game for three years." Cole moved over on the ottoman and patted the space for her to sit.

Madison sat on the edge near Clyde. "Really?"

"Yeah, it's serious stuff around here." Rod laughed. "We've been playing ever since I was old enough to move the pieces. I think Pop here had hopes of me becoming a champion chess player like he was in his day." Rod pointed to the long line of chess trophies lining the ledge above the chess table.

"You won all of those?" Madison admired the long line of accomplishments.

The older gentleman nodded and placed his cigar in the holder. He narrowed his eyes toward the chessboard. "Are you sure you want to move there?"

"Not anymore." Rod laughed. He studied the board and scratched his chin. He shrugged. "I'm not seeing whatever you are dad."

The old man chuckled. "Okay. I gave you a chance." He winked at Madison and moved his Queen to take Rod's King. "Check Mate."

Rod stared at the game board in disbelief. "Seventy-two years old, and his mind is sharper than a twenty year old." He picked up his King and laid him sideways on the board. He patted his dad on the arm. "Good game. We'll start a rematch after dinner. I think I hear Natalie and Nick."

Clyde pulled back the curtain at the window and smiled. "Finally, we can eat." He smiled.

The door opened and Rod's sister Natalie entered, her arms full of freshly baked pies.

Rod took them from her. "I'll take those." He pulled back the tin foil on one and stuck his finger in the meringue of the lemon pie.

"Rod, stop that. No one's going to want to eat that after you touch it." His sister pointed a coat hanger at him.

"Exactly. Mmm." Rod licked his finger and grinned.

Natalie shook her head and laughed. She hung her coat in the closet and kicked off her boots.

"Natalie, please meet Cole Harris and Madison Grey from *Women's World Quarterly*." Rod did the introductions.

"It's a pleasure to meet you both." She smiled. "I'm a huge fan of your work." She turned to Cole. "Although, I don't think even a fantastic photographer like yourself can make this old guy look good." She teased her brother.

"Hey, we're three minutes apart—and *you* were born first." Rod called over his shoulder as he carried the pies into the kitchen.

"That's not how I remember it." She laughed.

Clyde stood and hugged his daughter.

"Hi, dad." She gestured toward the chessboard. "Let me guess, your queen took his king in position eight?" She tucked her arm around the older man's waist.

"Yup. He made the mistake you predicted he would." Clyde chuckled. "Where's Nick and the kids?"

"Getting their skates sharpened. We took separate cars because I had to work late. The boys are excited about the skating party tonight."

"Skating party?" Cole's eyes widened.

"Yes, it's one of the highlights of the season's festivities. The *Town Center Park* is transformed into a magical ice palace with thousands of white lights. They set up a portable ice rink and booths where they serve hot chocolate and cookies and provide skate rentals, so don't worry if you didn't bring any."

"I love skating. That sounds great." Madison gained another surprised look from Cole. She suspected he found her sudden change of heart strange. She couldn't fully understand it. *Maybe it had something to do with him. Or* a lot *to do with him.*

"I'll probably be too busy taking pictures to skate." Cole shoved his hands in his pockets, avoiding Madison's gaze.

*Hmm…*Her eyes narrowed as she studied him. *I bet he can't skate.*

* * * *

Madison gasped as they rounded the corner onto *Main Street,* and the *Town Center* came into view. The trees surrounding the lake were strung with sets of white and blue lights flickering to the beat of Christmas carols. Miniature pole lamps lined the pathway around the lake. The booths Natalie had mentioned were made of

Styrofoam blocks, designed to look like ice huts, each labeled with signs that read hot chocolate, cookies and skate rentals. Traditional Christmas songs played over a loud speaker, and the three young boys sang along to *Rudolph the Red Nose Reindeer*.

"You know Rudolph isn't the only reindeer." Rod pouted.

The boys laughed and dashed off to put on their skates.

"Shall we get skates?" Madison asked Cole when they reached the edge of the frozen lake.

"I wish I could, but I should probably get to work." Cole held up his tripod and camera. He'd been clutching his camera bag since they'd left the Livingston home.

"Maybe later?" Madison's eyes narrowed with suspicion.

"Of course." He nodded.

"Okay, I'm going to head out with the others. I'll see you out there in a bit?" She grinned.

"Yeah, sure." His tone was noncommittal as he watched the skaters with a look of admiration mixed with terror. The faster they skated or the more complicated a stunt they landed the more Cole looked ready to faint.

Madison hid a giggle and turned away, leaving him to set up his camera.

A cheery old man wearing a Santa's hat greeted her inside the igloo hut. "Nice to see you again." He beamed.

It was the same man she'd seen at his costume fitting earlier that afternoon. *What was his name again? Archie...no Ernie.*

"Hi, Ernie. Can I please have a pair of size five men's skates?" Growing up in California, they hadn't gone ice skating much as kids, but they had roller-bladed quite a bit. After moving to New York, Madison had turned to ice skating as one of her favorite forms of exercise and had found men's hockey skates a similar fit and feel to roller blades.

"Sure thing." He searched the racks behind him and handed her the skates. "Do you need someone to tie them for you?" He gestured toward two teenage boys who were flirting with two pretty local girls. He shook his head. "Hey boys, get back to work."

The girls giggled and rushed off with their hot chocolate.

"Sorry dad." The taller boy said.

"Boys." Ernie took a deep breath and rolled his eyes. "Nothing but trouble." He grinned. "Do you have children, Madison?"

"No." Madison shook her head. She had wanted them once, but now she wasn't sure. Knowing how fast a marriage could end, she would hate to put children through that pain. For now she was content being *cool Aunt Madison* to Samantha's boys.

"Well if you decide to—don't have boys…" He looked toward the lake where a young girl was skating hand in hand with a much older boy. His eyebrows furrowed. "On the other hand, girls are not much better."

Madison glanced toward the skating couple and smiled. "Your daughter?"

Ernie nodded.

"Can Madison come and skate, Ernie?" Rod teased, poking his head inside the igloo.

"Oh yes. Sorry to keep you. Have fun." Ernie turned his attention to a family waiting for skates.

Madison followed Rod outside to the wooden benches. She sat and tugged off her boots. She slid her feet into her skates and wiggled her toes.

"Do you need a hand with those?"

"No, that's okay, thanks. My brother taught me how to tie skates years ago." Madison bent and started on the laces.

"Okay, when you're ready one of my old high school friends is back in town for the holidays, and I would like you to meet him. I've made him promise, no embarrassing stories or they might end up in print. In hindsight though, it was probably a bad idea to tell him not to. That may be enough motivation for him to reveal all." He chuckled and dashed off in the direction of his old classmate on the skating rink.

Madison pulled the leg of her jeans down over her skate and stood. She glanced toward the hot chocolate booth where Cole had set up his tripod. He snapped photos of the Livingston family on the ice rink, changing the lens several times. She didn't doubt the photos for the article would be amazing. *He* was amazing. Her feelings for him grew with each passing day, and she was anxious to see where things might lead once they returned to Staten Island.

"Madison, over here." Rod waved from the other side of the rink.

She waved and headed toward the two men.

Rod took her arm. "Madison, I'd like you to meet Chris Windsor, a pediatrician in New Jersey."

Chris smiled at Madison.

"Nice to meet you. So, how long have you two known each other?" She wished she'd thought of bringing her notebook along. She was having such a great time—she'd forgotten her purpose for being here. She vowed to work on her notes that evening.

"Too long." Chris grinned. "We grew up on the same street, went to the same schools…"

"Same little league baseball team in summer and triple A hockey team in winter," Rod finished. "Oh, you two will have to excuse me. I think Cole is flagging me over for a family photo." Rod skated to the other side of the rink where his family was positioned for a photo inside the gazebo.

"Shall we skate as we talk?" Chris asked.

"Sure." Madison pushed away from the boards and weaved in among the skaters. "Do you two keep in touch throughout the year?"

"Yeah. We make an effort to get together once a month…" Chris lowered his head and grinned. "When Rod isn't otherwise engaged." Chris struggled to keep up with her expert strides.

"What do you mean?" Madison slowed her stride.

"He doesn't know, I know, but my sister visits him often."

"Your sister?"

"Anita, from the bakery." He smirked. "Rod goes there for more than the baked goods, but for some reason whenever I ask him about it, he denies it." Chris shook his head. "My sister's been in love with Rod since we were in diapers. I think it's hilarious, they think I don't know."

Madison laughed. "That is funny. Why do you think they keep it a secret?" She glanced toward Rod who was posing for a picture with his nephews.

"Beats me." Chris shrugged, out of breath. "I just wish they'd get married and have a kid already. I'm dying to be an uncle." He paused and took a deep breath. "Okay, where did you learn to skate?"

"I used to roller blade on the beaches in California with my brother when we were kids, and the skating rink in Central Park is one of my favorite places to go during the winter months." She slowed her pace even more.

"You are certainly graceful on those men's skates." Chris matched her slower stride. "You live in New York?" He studied her.

"I live on Staten Island. The publication I work for has its headquarters there, and I like the quieter pace." Madison enjoyed the crisp air and the cool, refreshing wind on her face.

"I haven't been to Staten Island in years. Maybe in the New Year, I could take you to dinner."

The invitation took her by surprise, and she stumbled.

Chris grabbed her arm to steady her. "You okay?"

Madison skated toward the boards and moved away as she reached the edge of the rink. "Yeah, I'm good. Thank you." She smiled. Chris was a pleasant man, but the only man she was interested in having dinner with was Cole. She hesitated.

"So, what do you say—a friendly dinner and a tour around Staten Island?" Chris looked hopeful.

"Um…" Her eyes landed on Cole studying them from across the ice rink.

Chris followed her gaze. "Oh, I get it." He put his hands in his pockets. "Sorry, I didn't realize you two were together like that."

"Oh well, we're…" *What exactly?* They were no longer just co-workers, and she suspected the growing feelings she had for him were mutual. She smiled and shrugged. "Sorry, I can't have dinner with you."

"Fine, well at least skate around with me so I can tell you more embarrassing stories about Rod." He grinned. "There are many."

Madison nodded. "Okay."

* * * *

Cole stood and fought to keep his balance on the icy snow. His toes ached in the skates a half size too small, and his ankles felt weak as he walked through the tall snow banks bordering the ice's edge. *Why did people put themselves through this torture?* The balls of his feet were already seizing in muscle spasms. He stopped at the ice and watched as a group of school aged kids whizzed past. He frowned. *Show offs.*

He placed one foot on the ice and his leg stretched out in front of him. He teetered to keep his balance. *Forget, this.* Skating wasn't his thing.

He heard Madison laugh and turned his attention to where she skated alongside Rod's doctor friend. His eyes narrowed. *Okay, focus.* He could do this. It couldn't be that hard. Eight year olds were doing it.

He stepped out onto the ice. The ice surface felt like glass, and his arms flailed as he struggled to keep his footing. He took a deep breath. Madison and Chris had stopped skating and watched him from across the ice. He waved. "Whoa." He spun around and gripped the light pole on the bank. Waving was not a good idea. He steadied himself against the pole and straightened. He turned and lifting one foot after another made his way toward Madison. *Hey, this wasn't so bad.* He was staying on his feet at least.

Madison met him halfway. "How are you doing there? Or should I say, *what* are you doing?" She placed her hands on her hips and came to a stop in front of him.

"Skating." Cole studied his ice skates. Every muscle in his body tightened as he struggled to maintain his balance as the other skaters zoomed past him.

"That's not skating." Madison shook her head and giggled.

"It's how we skate where I come from." Cole lifted a foot and took another step.

"Florida?" Madison laughed.

"That's right, Florida." Cole grinned. "Now stop laughing and show me how to do this."

"Okay, stop moving." Madison stood behind him and placed her hands on the back of his hips. "On the count of three, gently glide your right leg across the ice, *without* lifting your skate off the ice."

He did as she instructed, and within a few minutes, he was gliding across the ice. He continued to struggle to keep his balance, but as Madison took his hand to skate next to him, his confidence grew, and the two were soon skating in the rotation with the other skaters.

"So, who was that guy I saw you skating with?" His tone was nonchalant.

"One of Rod's high school friends, Chris. He's a pediatrician in New Jersey." Madison repeated the few facts she'd learned in their short skate together.

"Was he flirting with you?" Cole grinned, a slight note of jealousy in his voice.

"Yes, I believe he was. He asked me to dinner." Madison brushed her long hair over one shoulder. She turned to look at him. "Why? Are you jealous?"

"Yes." His honesty earned him a look of shock. He glided to a stop in front of her. "I was insanely jealous, watching the two of you skate. You, looking amazing in that red scarf with your dark hair blowing in the wind behind you. Your sexy hips swaying with each glide. I had to be near you again. That's why I put on these ridiculous skates that are too small, so I could flirt with you and hopefully do a better job than that guy." He nodded in the direction where Chris skated alone.

Madison's breath caught in her throat. "Skating certainly isn't your thing. Maybe you should try something else."

Cole brushed her hair away from her cheeks and wrapped his arms around her waist, drawing her into his chest. "That won't be a problem."

"Cole—people are watching." Madison placed her hands against his chest.

Cole's grip on her waist tightened as he lowered his lips to hers. "So, let them think we're practicing for the Christmas play, Mrs. Cratchet," he whispered against her lips.

Chapter Eight

Madison lay awake, staring at the stucco ceiling of her room at the bed and breakfast. She'd tried reading, writing her article on the bachelors, watching the evening news, but thoughts of Cole, so close in the next room distracted her. She heard him get out of bed, and his footsteps echoed across the room. She suspected he couldn't sleep either. She fought the temptation to go see him. After the passionate kiss they'd shared on the lake, she wasn't sure she could trust herself alone with Cole.

Beep Beep

Her cell phone on the nightstand indicated a new text message. She opened the phone and read. *Are you asleep?*

Madison smiled. *No, I don't seem to be tired.* She hit *send* and waited for his reply.

Me neither…I can't stop thinking about you.

She hadn't been able to force him from her mind all evening. *I'm having a similar problem.*

What do you think we should do about it?

Madison hesitated. She could think of a few things. However, none of which she was entirely ready for. *I'm open to suggestions.* Her fingers flew over the keys. She bit her fingernail. *Was she?*

The reply was instantaneous. *Sleepover?*

Madison sat straighter on the bed. *Was she ready for this?* Her feelings for Cole were growing stronger by the day. With each thoughtful or caring gesture, he convinced her he was someone she could trust. His eyes revealed the depth of his emotions, and his lips melted her resolve. A sleepover could be dangerous. *Were they moving too fast?*

Her phone beeped with another message. *Had he changed his mind? Had he taken her silence as rejection?* She held her breath and opened it.

I only want to hold you, nothing more.

Okay, come over. Once the words disappeared into cyberspace, Madison ran to the bathroom to brush her hair and wash her face. She glanced at her blue satin nightgown. She tugged at the low-neck line and studied her reflecting in the mirror. *What was she doing?* They were coworkers on a business trip. She knew it was a lie. They'd become much more over the past ten days.

A soft knock on the door made her heart race. She tip toed to the door and opened it. Cole stood on the other side wearing a pair of men's grey pajama pants, tied at his waist. His bare chest gleamed in the dim lighting in the hallway. Madison's pulse quickened. *How was he was still single?*

Cole stepped inside and closed the door behind him. He took her into his muscular arms. "Oh, Madison," he whispered into her hair. He placed a trail of tiny kisses along her forehead and cheeks. He touched the tender spot where her bruise from the dashboard was starting to fade away. He kissed it gently.

Oh God, he smells good. It had been a long time since Madison had experienced the intensity of her body's reaction from the fresh from the shower manly scent. *Maybe this wasn't a good idea.* Cole's eyes, his touch and his kisses revealed he wanted to do much more than just hold her. *Would she let it go further than that? Would he try?*

Madison shuddered. "Cole…I…"

Cole silenced her with a soft kiss on her lips. "Shh…Let's try to get some sleep."

Madison gulped and nodded.

He took her hand and led her to the bed. He slipped under the covers and held them back for her to climb in. He wrapped her in his arms and pulled her into the curve of his body.

She rested her head on his chest and snuggled into his warmth. *How had she not realized she'd missed the warm, safe, comforting feel of a man's strong arms wrapped around her at night?* She hadn't let herself want it or need it. Kurt's arms had felt like a safe place at one time too. She pushed the thought from her mind. She refused to compare the two men.

Cole caressed her hair and traced his fingers the length of her bare arm.

She'd never be able to sleep with him doing that. Her heart raced, and sleep was the furthest thing from her mind.

Cole's fingers massaged her temples, relaxing her. Madison's breath grew heavy, and her body melted into the thick fleece sheets beneath her. Her eyes struggled to stay open, and she gave up the fight.

"Madison?" Cole's voice was low, whispering in her ear.

Was she dreaming his voice? "Hm?"

"I told you you'd want to spend more time with me once you got to know me." He chuckled.

A sleepy smile spread across her face as she snuggled closer to him. "You were right." He *had* been right about that. For so long she'd fought to keep men away from her. Yet this week no matter what she did, she found herself falling into Cole Harris's arms whenever they were alone and falling in love with him. Her body and her heart betrayed her any time she pushed him away. *Maybe it was time to stop pushing.*

* * * *

"So, don't forget to go to the bakery and pick up the pies I ordered for you both to take back to New York with you." Rod called from his driver's side window.

"We definitely won't, thanks again." Madison waved as she stepped onto the sidewalk outside of the bed and breakfast. The Christmas play had been a success, and now that it was over, so was their time in Tuscumbia. She'd stayed behind to help clean up and take down the play sets after the performance and exhausted after the long day, she yawned as she ascended the stairs.

Cole had disappeared once the play was over, claiming he had something to do. He'd asked her to join him for a late dinner in his room when she returned. She unbuttoned her coat as she made her way down the hallway to his room. She removed her coat and scarf and fluffed her hair before knocking on the door.

Cole opened the door and took her hand, dragging her inside. He wrapped one arm around her as he closed the door. "I've missed you." His warm breath against her neck made her shiver.

She giggled and moved away from him. "It's only been a few hours."

"Too long." He took her coat and ushered her into the room.

The sight in front of her took her breath away. A fresh cedar scented log burned in the wood fireplace along the stonewall. Garland and holly were draped over the mantle, and white lights hung in the window. Tiny tea light candles lit the room with a warm glow, and the distinct smell of Chinese food filled the air around them. The wine glasses on the table were filled with red wine. The view of the snow falling outside and the frost on the window enhanced the warm, cozy atmosphere. Soft, piano music played from the alarm radio on the bedside table.

Madison's stomach growled. "Wow, it smells wonderful in here."

"The food just arrived, your timing was perfect. Shall we?" Cole held out a chair for her.

"I am hungry." Madison sat and reached for her napkin. They hadn't eaten since that morning. It had been a busy day for both of them.

"Me too." Cole nodded, taking a seat across from her. "So, how do you think the play went?" He grinned as he opened the boxes of food.

"Good, I think. You were hilarious at the end when you forgot your lines and made up your own." Madison laughed. She spooned rice onto her plate.

Cole bit into a chicken ball. "I have to admit it was fun. I was terrified, but it wasn't as bad as I thought it would be." He took a sip of his wine and sat back in his chair studying her.

"Why are you staring at me?" Madison wiped her mouth with her napkin. "Do I have sweet and sour sauce on my face?" She licked her lips.

Cole shook his head. "I want to commit every inch of your face to memory. The way you look when the lights hit your hair and eyes—my God Madison—you have no idea what you do to me. I made a complete fool of myself in front of a whole town of people tonight, to see that smile of yours and I'd do it—or anything else for that matter—all over again. Anything to make you happy." He took her hand in his.

Madison swallowed an unexpected lump in her throat. She didn't trust herself to speak. She smiled at the man who had not only restored her Christmas spirit, but had shown her she could be happy again—in love again—with him.

"There is something else." Cole leaned forward, and his hands tightened around hers. He lowered his eyes to the table. "I want to talk to you about tomorrow."

Tomorrow? She gave him a puzzled look

"Meeting…the next bachelor." His eyes met hers.

Madison's face clouded. *Why was he bringing this up now?* They were having a great night. Her confession of love died on her lips as she sat back in her chair and waited for him to continue.

"I called Damien this morning, and I told him Kur…bachelor number five is your ex-husband, and how unfair it was to expect you to spend three days with him." Cole paused.

Madison studied the table. The plate of food swam before her teary eyes.

"He said he understood, and if we could find a replacement bachelor, he would consider the article anyway."

Madison's mouth dropped, and she pulled her hand away.

Cole reached for it again and held it in his own. "I made a few phone calls, and I know a guy on Staten Island who would be perfect. He's a real estate…"

"Stop." Madison interrupted. She didn't want to hear anymore. She'd heard enough. "You had no right to do that. If I had wanted Damien to know, I would have told him myself." Her tone remained even and steady. Inside, she was ready to collapse into tears. "Cole, I accepted this writing assignment to further my career. I won't let you ruin this for me." She fought to control her anger. *How could he have done this?* He hadn't even discussed it with her first.

"Ruin this? Madison he's your ex-husband who cheated on you. How can you look at him again?" His words stung.

"Who are you to talk about my former relationship? Something you know nothing about." She yanked her hand free and stood. She folded her arms across her chest. *This couldn't be happening.* The last thing she wanted was to have this conversation with him. Kurt's betrayal made her feel foolish and naïve. She didn't want Cole to see her that way.

"I know he was sleeping with a female co-worker behind your back and couldn't be bothered to be there for you on one of the most important nights of your life. When I saw you at that awards dinner three years ago, I thought you were the most beautiful woman I'd ever seen, and I thought your husband was a fool to not be by your side every moment." Cole stood and paced the floor. "Madison, please." He knelt on the floor beside her chair. "Don't do this. You don't have to."

"Yes I do!" Madison pushed past him. "I need to do this to prove to myself I am over him."

Hurt clouded Cole's face.

Why had she said that? Was it true? Did she need this to put Kurt and the past behind her and move on? She wished Cole could understand why she had to finish the assignment. It was more than the assignment. She needed to put an end to the numbness she'd felt for three years. The feelings of betrayal and hurt she never wanted to feel again. She had to do this, confront Kurt and her fears. "I don't expect you to come along." Madison picked up her sweater, and headed toward the door. Her heart ached and tears threatened to pour.

"I'll be damned if I'm letting you go there alone." He stood in front of the door. "You need someone to protect you from that man."

Protect her? Her eyes narrowed. "Is that what you think I need from you?" There was no more fighting them. Tears ran down her cheeks.

"Madison I didn't mean it that way." Cole's voice softened, and he wiped a tear.

She pulled away. This had gone too far. Her feelings for him, *their feelings for each other* had complicated the assignment. "You know, I think I may have made a terrible mistake letting this relationship become more than just a professional one." Her eyes met his, and she struggled to compose herself.

"Don't say that." Cole's eyes pleaded with her.

"Goodnight, Cole." Madison stormed out.

The moment her room door closed behind her, a fresh batch of tears started down her cheeks. She threw her sweater in a chair near the bed and kicked off her shoes. She couldn't believe him.

Calling her boss? Protect her? She was a grown woman. She could take care of herself. Anger mixed with hurt and sadness. She'd been so stupid to let him into her life and her heart. Hadn't she learned anything from her relationship and consequent divorce from Kurt? She shook her head. That wasn't fair. Cole was nothing like Kurt. He was kind, thoughtful, and loyal. She sighed. He wanted to protect her. While, the thought infuriated her, she softened.

Cole's door slammed down the hall.

She stiffened, prepared for another argument, but his footsteps echoed on the stairs instead. When she heard the door of the bed and breakfast close, Madison moved to the window.

Her room was dark except for the light from the Christmas lights draped across the mantle of the fireplace. He couldn't see her. He walked down the sidewalk, head down against the blowing snow. A block away he turned back.

She held her breath. *Had he changed his mind? Would he come to her? Did she want him to?*

Cole turned and stalked away.

Madison grabbed a blanket and sat on the window seat. She rested her head against the cold pane of glass. She closed her eyes, wishing she'd never accepted this assignment. She'd finish it. She had no other choice. Then she'd put this whole experience behind her, all of it, including Cole Harris.

Chapter Nine

Madison took a sip of her coffee. The hot liquid burned her mouth. She put the mug back on the table with a shaky hand and glanced around the café. *Where was he?* She checked her watch. 12:02. Two minutes late. She didn't have all day to wait. She drummed her fingers against the wooden table and fought to control her frazzled nerves.

Her breath caught in her throat as she saw him rush down the sidewalk through the frosted window. Kurt Davidson was a man who could make a woman's pulse race. At thirty-eight he was sexy in a distinguished, established sort of way. In his overcoat and navy scarf, he belonged on the pages of *GQ magazine*. Despite his infidelity splashed across page four of the business section in the New York Times, his law firm was still one of the most successful in the city, and she suspected his love life hadn't suffered from the bad publicity. *Why did women always think they could be the one to change a man?* In hindsight, the writing had been on the wall. She'd chosen to ignore it.

The bell above the coffee house door chimed behind her, and she held her breath.

"Madi, hi."

She stiffened at his informal use of her nickname. *How dare he call her Madi?* She sighed as her eyes met his. "Hello, Kurt."

He removed his coat and let his scarf hang around his broad shoulders over his crew neck tan sweater.

Dammit, he looked fantastic. Why couldn't he have gotten old or haggard looking? Or fat?

"I thought a photographer was coming with you?" Kurt scanned the cafe.

The mention of Cole made Madison's heart sink. The flight from Tuscumbia had been strained and awkward. They'd said little, and Cole had slept on the plane. Since they'd de-boarded in New York she hadn't heard from him, and she wasn't sure if he intended to be there at all. A part of her wished he wouldn't be.

She wasn't sure she could handle them both in the same place at the same time.

"He should be here later." Madison lied. "If we have to, we'll use the stock photos of you we have on file." She wondered how Damian would react to Cole abandoning the assignment. Probably not well.

"I'm relieved we have some time alone." Kurt toyed with the lid on her paper coffee cup.

Madison slapped his hand and moved the cup out of reach. She shot him an annoyed look.

"Madison, I'm sorry." His eyes refused to meet hers as he studied his folded hands.

Madison stiffened. *Sorry? Really? That's it after three years of nothing.* She'd avoided any attempt he'd made to contact her, never wanting to hear his excuses. She didn't want to hear them now. This assignment was already complicated enough. Did other writers find themselves in situations like this one? Maybe that was how tragedies were written—or murder mysteries.

"Madison, I…"

"Kurt, don't." She shook her head and held a hand out for him to stop. "Let's just think of this as an unfortunate coincidence and get through these few days as painlessly as possible. We're both adults." Madison folded her hands to keep them from shaking. Another few minutes and she could leave—at least for now. Being with him was harder than she'd anticipated.

Kurt's eyes met hers. "Coincidence? Madison, I refused to do this interview with anyone else. When Damien called to arrange it, he was sending another woman from the office, but I insisted he send you." Kurt leaned forward, resting his elbows on the table in front of him.

Madison blinked. His words didn't register. He'd been responsible for her getting this assignment? This assignment had gone from bad to wonderful to a complete disaster in such a short period of time. Damien hadn't intended to give her the assignment. She'd only been offered it to secure the interview with the fifth bachelor. She prayed it wasn't true, but she suspected it was. That realization stung.

"I wanted a chance to see you before I left. I'm moving to Boston to open another law office. " Kurt's voice beamed with pride at the news.

She stared at him, a blank expression on her face. *Was she supposed to care?* She sipped her coffee, fighting to compose her rattled nerves.

He leaned across the table to touch her arm. "You have avoided any attempt I've made to contact you. I've missed you a great deal, Madison."

The heat of his hand burned into her flesh, and an image of that hand caressing his receptionist flashed in her mind. She brushed his hand away and stood, gathering her coat. "Save your apologies, Kurt. They are about three years too late. Promise me we will not discuss anything that has to do with us or our past anymore. You've agreed to do this interview, I expect, you will go through with it?" She wasn't sure. She waited.

Kurt cleared his throat and nodded. "Of course. I understand."

"Great." Madison's heart beat loud in her ears, and she prayed he couldn't see how much he'd upset her. She opened her notebook, struggling to control her unsteady hands. "My file says you have a formal function tonight. What is it?" A formal function didn't sound too bad. She could go, observe long enough to gather a few notes, snap a few photos herself if necessary and then leave. She just had to collect enough information in the next three days to write a thousand words about him. And not the thousand that had come to mind these past three years.

He sat back in his chair and took a deep breath. "The company Christmas party."

Just when she thought things couldn't get worse.

* * * *

"You're not planning to go, are you?" Samantha's tone was one of disbelief on the other end of the phone.

Madison sank lower into a bubble bath, cradling her cell phone against her ear. "I don't know if I have a choice." She sighed.

"Of course you do. This is ridiculous. I think you've been a trooper about this assignment all along, but enough is enough. What if *she's* there?"

Madison grabbed her razor from the side of the tub and ran it along her leg. "Maybe that's one of the reasons I should go. To face them both. Show them I don't care anymore." Presented with the options of fight or flight, she'd readily choose flight. She wanted nothing more than to avoid seeing Kurt and his co-worker, whom she'd already seen too much of. But it would mean not finishing the article she'd set out to write. There wasn't an option. She had to go to the party and prove to everyone what she'd been claiming. She was over her ex-husband and she was a professional journalist.

"I guess." Samantha was reluctant to agree. "I just think you've been through enough." Her tone softened. "Have you spoken to Cole?"

"No." She'd left a message at the front desk for him about the party that evening, but she wasn't sure if he was even staying at the hotel. She hadn't heard him in the room next to hers so far that afternoon.

"I'm sure he'll come around." Samantha's tone was reassuring.

Madison had her doubts. She'd told him she'd made a mistake falling for him. It wasn't true. She closed her eyes and leaned her head against the bathtub pillow. *How had life gotten so complicated in two weeks?* "Maybe, but right now I need to focus on finishing this assignment and getting back to Staten Island before anything else can go wrong." She pulled the plug on the tub. She glanced toward the clock on the bedside table. 6:47. The party was in an hour.

"And you're sure about this? I can't talk you out of it?"

Madison shook her head.

"Madison, are you shaking your head or nodding? You do know I can't see you right?" Her friend's tone was light.

Madison smiled for the first time that day. "I'm nodding, then shaking my head. I have to do this."

"Okay, well, I've only got one other thing to say."

"What's that?" Madison held her breath, hoping for some much needed advice on how to live through seeing her ex-husband with another woman.

"Look hot."

Madison laughed and shook her head. "That's it? That's your advice?"

"Yes. Can you think of better advice given the circumstances?" Samantha laughed.

Madison thought for a moment. "No, I can't." She glanced toward her suitcase. The bag of samples from the *Gucci* photo-shoot lay on top. The red velvet dress peeked through the handle of the bag. *Hmm...could she pull it off? Only one way to find out.* "Sam, I gotta go. There's a too tight red velvet gown I need to squeeze myself into."

"That's my girl."

* * * *

Kurt's law office was located in a building in the center of *Times Square*. The fabulous upper floor suite of the fifty-floor skyscraper had an amazing view of the city. Madison stepped from the elevator into the main foyer of the office.

A young red haired girl she didn't recognize greeted her from behind the reception desk. "Are you here for the Davidson Miller Law Christmas party?" She held out a flute of champagne.

Madison accepted the glass and nodded. She'd need more than one of these half-filled glasses to get her through the evening.

"Coat check is down the hallway to the right. Enjoy." The young girl smiled and turned her attention to an older couple entering the foyer.

The office party décor had a winter wonderland snow globe theme. White lights and glistening frosted ornaments hung from the ceiling and soft fake snow fell in swirls to the floor. They'd spared no expense for this party. Business must be doing well. She scanned the dimly lit room. Other than a few senior executives, she didn't recognize the other faces. She let out a sigh of relief. No doubt the woman she was desperate to avoid had been forced to resign once the office affair had gone public. Her shoulders relaxed as she took another sip of her champagne.

"There you are." Kurt appeared next to her in the entryway. "Here, let me take your coat." He reached for her coat.

Madison cleared her throat. "Um—I'd rather keep it on. It's a little cool in here." Suddenly the red velvet dressed didn't seem like a great idea. What had she been thinking to wear something so revealing?

"I'll ask someone to adjust the heat, but I have to insist on taking it. Security measures." He shrugged.

Security measures? If she was planning to hurt him, she'd have done it three years ago. She pouted and removed the coat. "Fine, here." She handed him the coat and scarf and folded her arms across the tight fabric at her waist.

Kurt let out a low whistle. "Wow, you look stunning." He stepped back to take in the full extent of the dress. "How come I never saw this dress before?" His eyes twinkled with delight.

The appreciation she saw on his face as his eyes traveled the length of her body annoyed her. Her stomach turned. "Why? If I'd worn more dresses like this, would you have been able to keep your hands off of your receptionist?" She cocked her head to the side and bit her lip, wishing she could take the words back. Hadn't *she* been the one to suggest they leave the past in the past?

Kurt's grin faded. He cleared his throat and ran a hand through his sandy brown hair. "Should we get a drink? Dinner will be announced shortly."

"Yes, thank you. I won't be staying long." She needed to observe enough for the sake of the article, and then she could leave.

Kurt led the way through the crowded room to their table. "By the way, your photographer friend called this afternoon. He said he would be arriving later tonight."

Madison's heart skipped a beat. Cole would be there, after all. Apprehension mixed with excitement. She wanted so bad to see him, but the thought of Kurt and Cole in the same room together made her head ache. Cole hadn't concealed his feelings about her ex-husband, and Madison's brow wrinkled with concern. *What would happen once the two men met?* Had Cole decided to put his personal feelings aside for the assignment as well? She hoped so.

"There's a few people I need to greet. Are you okay here alone for a few minutes?" Kurt looked uncomfortable in her presence.

She'd been okay alone for three years. She bit her tongue to hold back the words. *Moving on, leave the past in the past.* She forced a smile. "Of course." She took her seat, aware of the eyes of Kurt's colleagues on her.

Kurt disappeared in the crowd.

Madison scanned the room for Cole. He didn't appear to be there yet. *Maybe he'd changed his mind?* She picked up her champagne flute and drained its contents.

Kurt's laughter on the other side of the room caught her attention. She turned in her chair to study him. He stood among a group of men she recognized from the law firm. One patted him on the back, and a wide grin spread across his handsome features. Part of the anger she felt melted away. *Maybe three years was long enough to be angry. After all she no longer had feelings for him, what would it hurt to forgive and forget?*

The waiter appeared and refilled her champagne glass.

"Thank you." She smiled.

"Glad to see you're avoiding the red wine," a deep, familiar voice said to her right.

A slow smile spread across her face as she turned to look up at Cole. Wearing a black suit and red dress shirt and tie, he looked even more handsome than she'd seen him. "Hi. I wasn't sure you were coming."

Cole pulled out a chair next to her and sat. He placed his champagne glass on the table. "I wasn't sure I was either." He studied the table and played with the stem of his glass.

"I'm glad you're here." She was glad. Having him by her side gave her the strength she would need to make it through the next few days. Her eyes met Cole's, and the heavy weight she'd struggled beneath all day disappeared. The love and kindness she found in him were more than she could have hoped for.

"I'm sorry about the other night." He took her hand in his under the table. "I shouldn't have interfered."

"No, you shouldn't have, but I understand why you did." Madison squeezed his hand. "I'm sorry too."

"What are we all apologizing for over here?" Kurt appeared behind them at the table.

Madison pulled her hand free of Cole's, and her cheeks blushed. *Why did she feel like she'd been caught doing something wrong?* "Kurt Davidson, this is Cole Harris." She made the introductions with a shaky voice.

Kurt extended a hand, and Cole stared at it.

Please shake his hand. Don't make a big deal out of this. Madison pleaded with her eyes. She held her breath.

"Pleasure." Cole extended his hand and stood. "I think I'm in your seat." He took his glass from the table.

"Thank you. Please, do join us." Kurt gestured toward an empty seat on the other side of the table.

They announced dinner and relief flooded through Madison. That went better than she'd expected. Maybe this wouldn't be so hard after all.

Kurt sat and leaned toward Madison. "So, tell me, how do you enjoy living on Staten Island?"

The waiter arrived and set their plates in front of them. The smell of basil and garlic drifted from the chicken and seasonal vegetables. Madison picked up her fork and speared a piece of broccoli. "It's quieter than the city, but I love it." It was true. Her life on Staten Island was much better than she'd expected when she'd escaped the city three years before.

"And the magazine? Are you writing many assignments?"

When had he become interested in someone else's career? She studied his expression. Genuine interest lay behind his gaze. "*Women's World* is fantastic. I'm mostly editing." She didn't tell him he'd been responsible for securing her first writing assignment.

"But your passion is writing." He bit into his chicken.

Madison almost dropped her fork. He *had* been paying attention. "Yes, and I haven't abandoned that." She refused to tell him about the manuscript she was working on. There was no way he'd remember that. She'd only started writing it in their last few months together.

"Did you ever finish the book you were writing?"

Madison's mouth fell open. Out of the corner of her eye she noticed Cole watching the interaction. A frown clouded his blue eyes. She didn't know what to say. "Um…how do you remember that?"

Kurt's dark eyes burrowed into her own. He leaned closer and whispered. "I remember everything about you, Madi."

* * * *

Cole sat back in his chair as the waiter took his plate. The scene across the table from him made his blood boil. He clenched his silk napkin in his fist and forced himself to look away. The dirt bag was worse than he'd thought. Pretending to be interested in Madison's career and turning on the charm. He could see why the man was successful in persuading women to trust him. He was a master manipulator. Madison had to know that by now, didn't she?

Her laughter caught his attention, and he turned to see them stand. Madison shook her head, but Kurt ignored her protests, dragging her onto her feet. The sight of her in the red dress took his breath away once again, and he frowned as he saw Kurt lead her out onto the dance floor.

She shot him a helpless glance and shrugged as they disappeared into the sea of couples on the floor. A musical rendition of *I'll be Home for Christmas* played from the speakers in the corner of the room, and Cole sighed as he slumped in his chair and loosened his tie.

"Want to dance?" A young woman to his right asked, leaning closer to him.

He'd noticed her watching him throughout dinner. This situation was awkward enough. He didn't need to ward off any advances of his own. He shook his head. "Uh…no thanks. I'm not much of a dancer."

"It'll get you closer." The woman nodded toward the dance floor.

Closer? Cole cocked his head to the side and gave the woman a puzzled look. "I'm not sure what you mean."

"To keep an eye on your girl." The woman smiled and stood. She came toward him, hand outstretched.

"Oh, I'm sure she can take care of herself." He glanced toward the floor where he could see the open back of Madison's dress. She'd said so herself. The last time he'd interfered, it had backfired in a way he hadn't planned. It was best to stay out of it. Madison was too smart to fall for her ex-husband's lies. He hoped.

The woman laughed and placed her hands on her slender hips. She studied the dancing couple. "I wouldn't be too sure." She gestured toward Madison and Kurt, as Kurt's hands slid lower on the small of Madison's back.

Cole let out a deep breath. "Okay, let's go." He followed the woman out onto the dance floor, positioning himself close enough to watch them.

"I heard Madison say, you're a photographer?" The woman wrapped her arms around his neck, and her hips swayed to the music.

Cole nodded, his gaze on Madison. He couldn't hear what she was saying, but her face was flushed, and she'd placed her hands against Kurt's chest, keeping a distance between them.

"I'm thinking about getting new photos taken in the spring for my portfolio…"

The woman's voice faded in the background, as he watched Kurt draw Madison closer to his chest. His hands moved further down her back. Anger cursed through him. *Why wasn't she stopping him?*

"What do you think?" The woman looked up at him.

Cole frowned. "Huh?" He stopped rotating.

The woman laughed. "About a photo shoot?" She gripped his shoulders, forcing him to turn with the music.

"Oh, yeah sure. I'll give you a business card." From the corner of his eye, he saw Madison and Kurt stop dancing. Madison had turned, and her back was pressed against her ex-husband. Kurt had a firm grip on her shoulder, and one arm squeezed around her waist. Madison struggled against his hold. Her eyes searched the room frantic, and she wiggled to free herself. *Okay, that's enough.* "Excuse me. I'm sorry…" Cole freed himself from the woman's embrace and made his way across the dance floor.

A look of relief spread across Madison's face as he approached, but she held a hand out in protest of his help.

He ignored it. "Let her go." He glared at Kurt.

A smug smile spread across the other man's features. "This doesn't concern you."

"From where I was standing it appeared the lady does not want to continue dancing with you, let her go." Cole took Madison's arm.

Kurt released her. "Fine. She's all yours." His arms fell away from Madison, and she stumbled toward Cole.

She shot him a grateful look.

"Are you done? Can we get out of here?" He stared into her teary eyes.

Madison looked between the two men. "What about the assignment?" She bit her bottom lip and clenched her lips together.

"You have to be kidding." Cole shook his head. "Do what you want Madison. I'm out of here." He held his hands up in defeat. If she wanted to stay and spend more time with this jerk, there was nothing more he could do about it, but he'd be damned if he was going to watch.

* * * *

Madison watched Cole's disappearing figure make its way through the crowded dance floor. She fought the urge to follow him. If he wanted to leave, he could leave, but this assignment was important to her. She'd made it this far, and the night was almost over. She forced a deep breath and forced herself to face Kurt. "What was that?" Anger made her cheeks flush.

"I'm sorry, I got carried away." He moved closer and pulled her back into his embrace as a new slow song started. "We have a history together. Do you think it's been easy for me without you, these past three years? I loved you. I still love you."

Madison broke free of his tight hold on her. She rubbed her forehead. *This was too much.* The champagne made her head feel light, and she swayed as she took a step backward. "I'm going to go."

"No problem. Let me grab our coats…"

She held a hand out to stop him. "No, you shouldn't leave. This is your party. I'll grab a taxi back to the hotel and meet you tomorrow." The idea didn't appeal to her, especially the idea of sitting in a courtroom all day. Apparently Kurt's Christmas traditions were no different from his everyday life. He was certainly the work-a-holic among the group. Maybe she'd have time to write her article to keep from falling asleep during the legal proceedings.

"No way. It's late. I'm not letting you leave alone." He took her hand, ignoring her protests and made their way to coat check. He handed their coat check stubs to the young man sitting behind the counter.

"Really I'm fine." She was used to doing everything alone. Catching a taxi at nine o'clock was not a big deal. She took her coat from the coat checker. "Thank you."

Kurt handed the young man a large tip and helped Madison slide into her coat. "Forget it Madi." He tossed his own overcoat over his arm and wrapped his scarf around his neck. "Let's go. My car and driver are waiting out front."

His car and driver? An image of *Mr. Big* from *Sex and the City* flashed in her mind. *How had she not have been put off by his pretentiousness before? Had she been that gullible?* His money had never impressed her. It had been his charm and gentle persuasion that had captivated her. She knew better this time.

He hit the button for the elevator, and Madison slid her hands into her leather gloves.

"What's going on between you and Cole? A little office romance?"

He'd know about that wouldn't he? She bit her tongue. "I don't want to talk about it." She looked away and watched the numbers light up.

"Let's hope he's not the fool I was." Kurt opened the door on the Main floor of the office building and ushered her outside.

Madison remained silent as she slid into the backseat of the black limo.

Kurt slid in next to her. "The *Roosevelt Hotel,* please."

Madison stared through the tinted windows, watching the bustling New York streets whiz by as they drove the few blocks to the hotel.

Kurt touched her hand on the seat. "You know, it really is great to see you."

The car pulled up in front of the hotel.

Madison moved her hand and unclasped her seatbelt. "Thanks for the ride. I'll see you at the courthouse tomorrow." Her hand searched for the door. She had to get away from Kurt and his piercing dark eyes. Something about him entrapped her. She didn't love him, and the truth about who he was made her ill, yet her pulse raced when his hand touched her cheek. She wiggled the handle, desperate to escape the confines of the car. The door was locked.

Kurt moved closer, resting his arm across her shoulders. He leaned toward her, and his lips brushed against her neck.

Stop it. She didn't like the way her body reacted to his touch, his kiss. Her stomach turned and anxiety crept into her chest. She pushed him away and tapped on the glass for the driver. "Can you unlock the door, please?"

The door clicked open. She opened the door.

Kurt grabbed her arm. "Why don't I come upstairs with you?" He stroked her arm. "I'm sure I can give you better material to write about than that photographer." He smirked.

The sight of his smug look infuriated her. She tugged her arm free and seconds later her hand made contact with the side of his face. *That felt good.* She smiled. *Assignment complete.*

Chapter Ten

Madison climbed the icy stairs to Samantha's front door. She rested the stack of presents against her hip and rang the doorbell. A glance at her watch revealed it was before nine, but she suspected her friend would be up. With three young boys, sleeping in on a Saturday morning was a rarity.

"Madison? What are you doing here? You weren't due back until the twenty-second." Samantha swung the front door open in surprise. She wrapped her robe tighter around her body and squinted as the early morning sun reflected on the snowy front yard.

"You look like you were sleeping." Madison gave an apologetic look. "Did I come at a bad time? I thought the boys woke early…"

"The boys spent the night at their grandparent's house." Samantha yawned.

"Oh, I'm sorry Sam. Go back to sleep. I'll come back later." Madison shifted the weight of the presents in her arms.

Samantha shook her head. "No way, don't be silly. Come on in. I'm dying to know what happened." She stood blocking the entrance.

"Why don't you let her inside, so she can tell you?" Samantha's husband, Mike appeared behind her at the door. "Good morning, Madison. I hope one of those are for me." He gestured to the presents.

Samantha shot her husband a look. She stepped back and dragged Madison inside. "I'll start the coffee, and then I want to hear everything that happened."

"Coffee would be wonderful." She'd already consumed a pot that morning, but the caffeine was a necessity. Sleep had eluded her the night before.

"Okay. Have a seat in the living room. I'll be right back." Samantha dashed into the kitchen.

Madison set the presents under the big Christmas tree in the living room and removed her coat and gloves. She sat in her favorite plush armchair close to the fireplace and curled her legs beneath her.

Samantha emerged with two steaming mugs of coffee and a plate of toasted bagels.

Great, carbs. With the way she was eating, she'd be lucky to have anything fit in the New Year. She sighed. The comfort food was too tempting to resist. She grabbed a bagel, as Samantha set the tray on the coffee table.

"Now tell me everything that happened since we last spoke. I take it the Christmas party didn't go well." Samantha helped herself to a cinnamon raisin bagel. She took a big bite and sat in the corner of her sofa, tucking a fleece blanket around her bare legs. She gave her friend her full attention.

Madison gave a wry smile. "Not at all." She bit into her bagel. She recounted the events of the night before. By the time she revealed, she'd ended the night by assaulting one of New York's top lawyers, she held the full attention of her best friend.

"Oh my God, I can't believe you did that. I mean, it was totally overdue, but I never thought…" Samantha shook her head in disbelief. She stared at her friend with newfound appreciation.

"I know." A grin spread across Madison's face. "It certainly felt good."

"What are you planning to do about the assignment?" Samantha asked.

"I haven't decided yet." Madison drained the contents of her coffee cup. She'd finished writing about bachelor number four that morning, but had no idea how to write about number five. She couldn't leave the article with four because the cover had already gone to the press announcing the article with a *five* bachelors theme. Not to mention, Damien expected a finished article. If she didn't deliver the story he was expecting, she doubted he would give her another writing assignment.

"If you need any help, I'm here." Samantha patted her hand.

A commotion outside the front door caught their attention.

"The kids must be back. Mike's mom and dad are going to Hawaii for Christmas and wanted to do Christmas morning with the boys this weekend." Samantha explained as they all entered the house.

"Aunt Madison!" The boys exclaimed seeing their favorite aunt.

"Did you bring presents?" The youngest boy, David, tugged at the edge of her sweater.

"Yes, she did." Mike joined them. He raised his eyebrows and clapped his hands.

Samantha rolled her eyes. "I don't know who's worse. The boys or Mike. Last week I caught him snooping for gifts in our closet. He had Jacob, *our six year old* as a lookout." She shook her head and looked at her husband. The love she felt for him clear in her eyes.

Madison felt a tug at her heart. She wondered if she'd ever find the kind of relationship her friends shared. She cleared her throat. "Okay, let's open some presents."

They all settled in around the Christmas tree, drinking eggnog and exchanging presents.

Samantha collected the discarded wrapping and bows. "By the way, Madison, why are we doing this now? Aren't you coming to Christmas day dinner?" She had the last two holidays, and it had become a tradition.

"Actually, I've accepted my parent's invitation to go see them in California after all. I think the sun would do me good." Madison helped David open his remote control car. She'd been contemplating her options all morning and visiting her parents was the most logical one. It was the only way she had any hope of forgetting about Cole. Well, maybe not forgetting about him, but at least being far enough away from him she wouldn't run into him during the holidays.

"When do you leave?"

"Tomorrow afternoon. If I can finish this article, I'll be going in to the office tomorrow morning, and then my flight leaves at two o'clock." Madison stood and stretched. She helped Samantha clean up the wrapping paper. "I guess I should go." She yawned and glanced at her watch. It was almost lunchtime. If she had any hope of finishing the article, she'd better get to work.

Arriving back at her apartment, the silence was louder than usual. Compared to Samantha's home filled with noise and laughter, a husband and children, Madison's world was empty. She gazed out her front window at the decorated trees in the yard. She should have at least gotten a Christmas tree. *Okay, no more procrastinating.* She forced herself to sit at her computer desk. She opened a new file and reread what she'd written of her article. *Not bad.* She sat back in her chair and chewed the end of her pen. *How was she supposed to finish it?* She couldn't write about her experience with Kurt. It lacked the *feel good* theme she was aiming for. *Hmm...* Damien had said if she could find a replacement bachelor for Kurt, he would still consider the article. *Who could she write about?* She closed her eyes and rested her head against the chair. An image of Cole's sexy smile and gentle laugh appeared behind her closed lids. A smile spread across Madison's face, and she opened her eyes. *Cole. Of course.* He was the *perfect* bachelor, and she knew him better than any of the others. He was a man so kind and caring any woman could fall in love with him. *She had, after all.* She sat forward in her chair, and her fingers flew across the keyboard. *Bachelor number five—Cole Harris.*

* * * *

Madison stared through the dirty taxi window as she rehearsed what she planned to say to Damien. Her email to him the night before had stated she was back early and needed to meet with him first thing in the morning. She hoped her article would impress him, and he would realize he'd been wrong not to have considered of her first to write it. *Choose your battles.* Her mother's favorite saying echoed in her mind. For the sake of her future with the magazine, she decided to let the issue slide.

She took a deep breath as she stepped off of the elevator on the fourteenth floor a half hour later.

"Come in Madison. How was the trip?" Damien didn't look up as she knocked on his open office door and entered the room. His desk was covered in pages of print requiring final proofing. Her absence from the office these past few weeks put them behind on the editing. She usually put in hours of overtime during deadline week.

"It was…" She searched for the right word. *Eye opening, wonderful, disastrous?* "Fine. I met some wonderful people."

Damien didn't respond. His red pen scribbled across a cosmetic ad in front of him.

"I have the article." Madison opened her briefcase. "It's not the way we discussed, but I think my replacement bachelor is better than the original." *By a long shot.* The two men couldn't be compared. Madison held the article out.

Damien looked at her and leaned forward. He took the article and laid it on a pile of clutter in his inbox. "Madison, I sent a backup story to the press an hour ago. I'm sorry but when I received your email last night that you were back early, I assumed you hadn't finished the interview with Kurt, so I sent Meghan's story to the press instead." He glanced back down at the stack of papers on his desk.

Madison's mouth fell open. She didn't know how to respond. Her knees felt unsteady, and her hands shook. She couldn't believe this. He had *expected* her to fail. All this time working for the magazine, putting in hours and hours of overtime, helping to come up with story ideas, which were always assigned to someone else, and accepting the worse writing assignment ever hadn't mattered at all to her boss.

When she didn't respond, he glanced at her. "Madison, you are a wonderful editor, but editors don't always make for good writers. Stick with what you know you are good at. *That* is the key to success." He smiled and returned his attention to the ad. "Now, if you wouldn't mind grabbing a stack of articles that still need…"

"Damien, I quit." Madison swallowed the lump in her throat. She refused to work for a man who didn't believe in her. She'd accepted the job as an editor for the opportunity to break into print herself, and she realized that wouldn't be a possibility at *Women's World Quarterly* magazine. This assignment had done nothing to further her career the way she'd hoped it would.

"Madison, be sensible. You don't want to quit." He picked up a stack of articles and held them out to her.

She ignored them. "The fitness season is coming up Damien, better start looking for a new editor." Madison turned and left his office.

The moment the elevator doors closed behind her, she sunk back against the wall. Never in her life had she made a hasty decision without thinking it through. *But what was there to consider?* She couldn't continue to work in a position that didn't offer her the opportunities she deserved.

She grabbed empty copy paper boxes from the storage room and packed her personal belongings. Having made the decision to quit, she wanted to leave the office as soon as possible. She cleared her bookshelf, packing away her collection of books on writing and editing. Over the years she'd gathered quite the collection of reference materials. She prided herself on the fact she'd read each and every one, soaking up new bits of information and helpful knowledge from each. She left her quarterly magazine issues where they sat on the otherwise empty shelves.

She stood on her office chair and removed her diplomas from the wall. She placed them in the bottom of a new box. She cleared the miscellaneous items from her desk, leaving just her silver nameplate. By the end of the week a different name would replace hers. Her mail still sat unopened on her desk, and a thin manila envelope toward the bottom of the pile caught her attention. The familiar logo on the corner of the envelope made Madison's heart thump louder than anything else she'd experienced that week. A letter from the publishing company where she'd submitted her manuscript months before.

Damien's comment echoed in her mind. *Editors didn't make good writers. Could he be right?* Madison hesitated. *Did she really need more bad news this week?*

Unable to resist, she tore open the envelope. *Dear Ms. Grey, we are pleased to inform you your manuscript has been chosen for publication.* The rest of the words swam on the page as Madison read on to find out they were willing to provide her with an advance during the editing process, and they were confident her book would sell. A senior editor had been assigned to the manuscript, and her contact information was listed toward the bottom of the page. No doubt the publishing house would be closed for the holidays, but she would contact her first thing in the New Year.

Madison took a few deep breaths to compose herself and folded the thick paper. The timing of the letter couldn't be better. Moments before, she'd quit her job with no plans of what to do next, and now her dream of becoming a published writer was coming true. Excitement bubbled inside.

She picked up her box of items and hit the light with her elbow as she exited out into the hallway. They were empty and quiet as she made her way to Samantha's office. The marketing and accounting staff had already left for the holidays, and Madison was glad to make a quiet, un-dramatic exit.

Samantha's desk was pile high with work, and her phone was cradled against her shoulder. Glancing up, she waved Madison inside. "Mike, you have to cut it out of his hair." She rolled her eyes. "If you wait until I get home, the gum may get tangled, and we are having their photos taken with the Santa Claus at the mall tonight." Her gaze settled on the box Madison held, and she frowned. "Mike, I'm sorry honey, but I have to go. I'll call you back." She replaced the receiver and stood. "What do you think you're doing?" she hissed as she closed her office door.

Her assistant, Sophie peered over her cubical wall, intrigued.

Samantha waved her back to work.

"Quitting." Madison set the heavy boxes on Samantha's desk. She was dying to tell Samantha about her manuscript acceptance letter, but she needed to deal with this part first.

"But Madison, you love your job. What happened in your meeting with Damien?" Samantha sat on the corner of her desk and studied her.

"He told me he didn't have confidence in my ability as a writer. He sent a backup article to the press this morning." Madison smiled.

"And you're not upset?" Samantha gave her a puzzled look.

"No." Madison shook her head. She would miss working with Samantha every day, but at least her new writing schedule would give them time to have lunch. Something they'd always been too busy for in the past.

"Why not? I'd be angry as hell." Samantha wore a look of disbelief.

"I was at first." Madison nodded. "But after reading this letter from *Malcolm and McMullan's Publishing House*, I feel much better." Madison took the letter out of the envelope. "Damien's entitled to his opinion of my writing capabilities, I'm just glad M and M publishing thinks differently." Madison handed the letter to Samantha, no longer able to contain the excitement she felt.

Samantha read the first line of the letter. Her eyes widened, and a smile spread across her face. She finished reading and handed the letter back to Madison. "That's wonderful. I'm proud of you." She hugged her. "We have to celebrate when you get back. When is that, by the way?"

"You know, I'm not sure. I *was* planning to come home after the New Year, but now I may stay in California a little longer. I can work on the book there as easily as I can at home, without distraction." *As usual she had no reason to be at home.* She pushed the sad thought away. *Today was a good day. Focus on the good.*

"Don't stay away too long. I still need my yoga partner." Samantha hugged her and congratulated her once more.

Madison wrote her parents' home number on a post it note and handed it to Samantha. "Just in case."

Samantha's assistant knocked on the door and opened it. She popped her head inside. "Ms. Grey, I have mail here for you," Sophie said.

"Please have it sent to Kim in Human Resources. She can give it to my replacement." Madison said to Sophie. She suspected Sophie had witnessed the scene in Samantha's office.

A look of curiosity appeared in the young girl's eyes. "But this one is addressed to you personally." Sophie handed Madison a large, thick, white envelope. It had been addressed to her, care of *Women's World Quarterly*. "A separate identical envelope arrived for the magazine as well."

"Thank you." Madison opened the envelope and pulled out its contents.

Samantha and Sophie watched.

Inside was an envelope of photographs. There was no letter attached, just a sticky note stuck to the top of the pile. *Merry Christmas, little lady. I thought you might like to have these. Cole.*

"They must be the photos he took of the bachelors." Madison told the girls. She flipped through the stack, and her mouth fell open. They were all of her making snow angels with the Thompson girls, modeling Gucci, skiing in Whistler and dressed as Mrs. Cratchet in Tuscumbia.

"I don't see any bachelors in those pictures." Samantha peered over her shoulder.

"Wow, Madison those photos are amazing. Did he take any of anyone else?' Sophie leaned on the desk to have a better view.

Madison gulped and forced a deep breath.

"You have to go see him. He loves you, despite what you think." Samantha wrapped an arm around her shoulder.

Madison placed the photos back into the envelope. Tears stung the back of her eyes and threatened to fall. "But I'm getting on a plane in four hours." She wanted nothing more than to go see Cole, especially now that she had wonderful news to share with him. He would be excited for her and proud she'd stood up for herself with Damien, but she didn't know how to face him after everything that happened between them.

"And you still can, but you can't leave without at least talking to him." Samantha reasoned.

Madison hesitated. *Would he want to see her?* She hadn't heard from him in two days. The silence and lack of communication was killing her, and she missed him. She took a deep breath. "You're right." She nodded. She had to see him. She couldn't leave without knowing where they stood. She prayed he did still love her.

"Here, why don't you wear my new scarf and glove set." Samantha handed Madison a dark blue scarf and mittens. Tiny white snowflakes covered the soft fabric.

A month ago, Madison would have refused to wear anything reminding her of Christmas, but now she liked the idea.

"Thanks Sam." She hugged her friend. "Wish me luck." She gathered her things.

"You don't need it. He loves you." Samantha smiled.

"I hope you're right." Madison didn't wait for the elevator. She ran downstairs and pushed through the revolving door of the building. "Taxi!"

* * * *

Cole sorted through his camera lenses on his workstation. *Where was the 105 mm lens?* He picked up his camera case and opened it. He rummaged inside and pulled out two different lenses. Neither was the missing lens. He rubbed his scruffy chin. He needed a shave. Some sleep wouldn't be bad either. He'd barely slept in the two days since seeing Madison. An image of her in Kurt Davidson's arms reappeared behind his closed lids whenever he tried to sleep. *What had happened after he'd left the party? Had Kurt talked his way back into her good graces? It didn't make sense.* He rubbed his temple. His head hurt. *Why had he agreed to do this photo shoot today?* Work was the furthest thing from his mind.

The young *Miss Teen Manhattan 2011* sat on his sofa, giggling into her cell phone. She couldn't be more than sixteen and already her modeling career was booming. She shut her cell phone and stood. "Are we ready to start? My boyfriend will be here to pick me up in an hour." She looked at the clock on the wall.

"Yeah, I'm just looking for a different lens." Cole scanned the studio. *Where the hell had he put that lens?* "I can't remember where I laid it." He placed his hands on his hips and frowned.

The young girl reached forward and pointed to the lens on the camera. "Is that it?"

Cole rolled his eyes. *Teenagers. Thought they knew everything.* He wasn't that absent minded. He would have remembered setting up the—the 105 mm lens sat on the front of the camera. He cleared his throat. "That one will have to do."

He positioned the backdrop and lights, and the young girl moved through the first set of photos. Taking pictures helped to ease his mind, and for the first time in days he was able to think about something else other than Madison. He snapped shot after shot until his cell phone rang. *Madison?* He lunged for the ringing phone on his end table. Erik Johnson's cell number blinked on the screen. He'd left the *Gucci* executive a voicemail message that morning. He was desperate to take him up on his offer. He couldn't imagine taking any more jobs at *Women's World*. Not now. Seeing Madison and not being able to hold her, or kiss her would be torture. More torture than not seeing her at all. He was grateful for this other opportunity. It would mean a lot of traveling, but there was nothing keeping him in one place. The thought depressed him. "I have to take this." He waved the phone in the air.

"No problem." The young girl didn't look up from the text message she typed on her iPhone.

Cole closed the screen doors to the studio and answered his ringing cell phone. "Erik, hi."

"Cole, I was pleased to receive your message this morning."

"I was hoping you were serious about offering me a job." Work would be his only escape. In two days he hadn't heard from Madison, and he was losing hope.

"Of course. I have a meeting with the other executives set up for this afternoon before we all take off for the holidays. I know it's short notice, but would three o'clock work for you at our downtown office?"

Cole glanced at the clock. Almost eleven. He caught a glimpse of his dishevelled appearance in his toaster. "Sure, no problem." He'd have to hustle. He heard the doorbell ring. *Must be the girl's boyfriend.*

"The address is…"

Cole grabbed a piece of paper and jotted down the information Erik gave him. "Great. See you soon."

* * * *

Two hours later, Madison sat in a taxi outside of Cole's studio loft in Manhattan. A quick call to his home on Staten Island had revealed he was spending the holidays at his studio. She couldn't help but wonder if he was trying to avoid seeing her, by escaping from the island the way she'd planned. Her courage waned. *Maybe this wasn't such a good idea.*

"Hey lady, are you getting out?" The taxi driver glanced at her through the rear view mirror.

Madison hesitated. "Um—yeah. Please wait for me for a few moments." Madison told the driver. "I won't be long, but if I am gone for more than ten minutes, you can leave." Madison didn't expect Cole to be happy to see her, but she had to try. He had sent her the photos after all. *Did she dare hope the action meant something?*

She rang the doorbell and waited. Footsteps approached the door, and her pulse raced. The last few days without him had been torture. She'd come to realize how much he meant to her. She missed him like crazy. Loved him like crazy.

"Can I help you?" A female voice asked.

Madison looked up to see a beautiful, tall, blonde girl, looking phenomenal in a pair of jeans and tank top. The same girl Madison had seen Cole talking to on the plane to Whistler, a few weeks before. She had a thick Australian accent.

"I was looking for Cole." Madison felt foolish. *Why was she here?* He made it clear how he felt that night of the Christmas party when he'd left her with Kurt. Now he was here spending the Christmas season with another woman, and it appeared she was interrupting something. The smooth sounds of Bob Marley's *Stir it up* came from inside the apartment. There were two reasons she could think of people listened to Bob Marley, and she didn't think there was a peace rally going on inside the studio.

"He is in the other room, a little busy at the moment. Do you want to come in and wait?" The girl frowned.

"Um—no, that's okay. I have to go, but could you let him know Madison stopped by to say, *Merry Christmas*. We worked together, that's all." The words were a lie. They'd become so much more. While she'd been desperate to keep their relationship a professional one, he had worked his way past her resolve and had found his way into her heart.

"Will do. Is that all?" She placed her hands on her slender hips and shivered from the cold breeze blowing through the front door.

Madison stared at Cole's beautiful houseguest and sighed. Cole was surrounded by attractive, young models whose attention he didn't have to compete for. She doubted he'd given her a second thought these past few days. "Yes, that's all." Madison forced a smile.

She climbed back in the taxi. "Airport, please." She swallowed the lump in her throat and wiped a tear from the corner of her eye. Emotionally exhausted she slumped against the seat. *Why had she fought so hard to keep him away, only to let him hurt her in the end? This was her own fault. Men like Cole could date any woman they wanted. Why hadn't she listened to her instincts?*

She stared out the window of the taxi, lost in her own depressing thoughts as they drove through the crowded streets of New York. The shops were full of people doing their last minute Christmas shopping, hurrying down the sidewalk in the heavy snowfall. The big, white flakes reminded her of the snow in Whistler as they collected on the ground. She almost didn't hear her cell phone ring in her purse. She answered the unknown number on the last ring. "Hello."

"Madison Grey?" A female voice asked.

"Yes, this is Madison."

"Hi, Madison. I'm Isabelle Morano, from M and M Publishing. The editor assigned to your manuscript. We wanted to touch base with you to make sure you were still interested in having your book published with us, as we hadn't heard from you."

Was she still interested? Were they kidding? "Oh yes, of course. I was out of town for work and received your letter today. It couldn't have come at a better time."

"Great. Well, we don't usually work over the holidays, but I thought if I could send you the notes I've already made on certain chapters of the book, that you might have some time to do revisions. I don't want to intrude on any holiday plans." Isabelle said.

"No, I have no plans at all." Her parents would understand. "I'd be happy to work on the book." It was an understatement. She'd been waiting a long time for this opportunity. Excitement eased some of the anguish she felt. The book had been a work in progress for years. Completing it had been a huge accomplishment. She couldn't wait to see it in print.

"Perfect. I'll have the notes sent to you this afternoon by courier." Isabelle said. "And Madison, welcome to the *Malcolm and McMullan Publishing* family."

"Thank you." She disconnected the call and paid the driver an extra twenty to turn around, and take her back to the ferry. Once again she would be spending the season alone in her apartment. At least she'd have the revisions to keep her mind occupied.

They turned the corner onto Main Street, and a familiar sign caught her eye. "Hey, could you stop there first." She pointed to the bakery on the corner.

The driver huffed and grumbled, but did as she asked.

French Kiss Cookies was one of the most popular bakeries in Manhattan, and they were famous for their comfort treats. If there was ever a time she needed them, it was now. Nothing could get her through the season like double fudge chocolate chip and oatmeal cookies. She might gain a few pounds, but who cares? She wasn't planning to leave her house for a while anyway.

She tapped her foot as she waited in the long line up to pay for her three-dozen cookies. The smell of the still warm chocolate and oatmeal was too tempting to resist. She opened the bag and pulled out a cookie. Chocolate melted on her hand, and she licked it clean. *Mmm…*

"Madison?" A deep voice said behind her in line.

Turning, she recognized the *Gucci* executive she'd met at the fashion shoot two weeks before in *Central Park*. She swallowed the lump of cookie. "Hi, Erik."

He glanced at the bag of cookies she held and grinned.

She blushed and shrugged. "I'm expecting a lot of company over the holidays."

Erik winked. "Don't worry. I eat at least a dozen of those cookies a week. It's impossible to walk past on the way to the office each morning without stopping in." He laughed. "Enjoying your new shoes?"

Madison smiled and nodded. No sense telling him she wouldn't be getting a chance to wear them for a while. She no longer needed to dress up to go to the office, nor did she have a social life where she could show them off. Maybe she could wear them around her house as she ate her three dozen chocolate and oatmeal cookies. An image of her in the three hundred dollar stilettos with a chocolate mustache dancing across her living room flashed in her mind, and she shuddered. Reserving a private study room in the Staten Island library might be a better place to work on the manuscript.

"You wouldn't happen to know anything about that, would you?" Erik was asking.

Madison gave him a blank look. *Had she missed something while daydreaming about her shoes and cookies?* "I'm sorry. Know anything about what?"

"Cole rushing out of our meeting with the other executives this afternoon. He came by to discuss his new contract with us for the spring. His cell phone vibrated a few times, and next thing he mumbled something about a woman he had to see, and he left. I don't know..." Erik shook his head, disappointed. "Anyway, you haven't seen him, have you?" He approached the counter. He took her bag of cookies and added it to his bill.

"Uh, thank you. And no, I haven't seen him." Madison struggled to hide her own disappointment. *He had mentioned a woman?* Her heart hit the floor. He was over her already. Not only did he have a beautiful woman in his apartment, but he was rushing off to meet another one? This didn't sound like the Cole she'd come to know and love. Her disappointment turned to anger. *How could he walk out of his meeting with the* Gucci *executives?* This would have been a huge opportunity for him. A chance of a lifetime to achieve the recognition he deserved as a photographer. His photos would appear in magazines all over the world. He would realize his dream of traveling as a photographer, and a signed contract would guarantee steady work. She clutched her paper bag and frowned.

"If you talk to him, please let him know I pulled some strings to smooth things over with the other executives, and we are still interested in working with him. Tell him to call me." He handed Madison a business card.

"I will." Madison tucked the card into her wallet though she doubted she'd be seeing Cole anytime soon.

"Thanks. Have a wonderful Christmas. Don't eat all of those cookies yourself. We may need you to model again sometime." Erik winked and waved as he left the bakery.

* * * *

Madison closed the taxi door and handed the driver his fare through his open window. "Merry Christmas."

The driver waved, his mouth full of chocolate oatmeal cookie as he drove away.

"You're back?" Her landlord, Frank was perched high on a ladder changing the burnt out bulbs in a string of colored lights hanging from the bare maple tree on the front yard. "I thought you would be halfway to California by now." He tossed an old bulb toward the trash can beside the building. It missed and landed in a snow pile.

"Change of plans." Madison bent to pick up the bulb and tossed it into the can. "I decided to stay home to work on my book." She smiled. Now that her manuscript had been accepted, she wanted to tell the whole world. For now, she had to start with Frank.

"You're writing a book?" He raised his eyebrows.

"Yes." Madison dragged her heavy suitcase up the slippery driveway. The snow fell in swirls around them, and the air was chilling as the sun set. Maybe she should have gone to California.

Frank shimmied down the ladder. "Here, let me help you." On the middle rung of the old ladder he lost his footing and crashed to the icy ground at her feet.

"Frank! Are you okay?" Madison rushed to help him stand, trying not to lose her own footing on the slippery walkway.

"Yeah, yeah. I'm fine." He blushed as he dusted snow from his jacket. "Just a little dizzy." He sat on the front steps of the apartment building.

"Okay, sit here and relax." Madison laid a hand on his shoulder, steadying him as he swayed.

"Oh, before I forget, there was a guy here looking for you about twenty minutes ago." He blinked struggling to focus, and he rubbed the back of his head.

A guy? The courier with the manuscript? "Was it a delivery?"

Frank frowned and thought for a moment. He shook his head. "No, I don't think so. At least, he didn't leave any packages or anything."

Madison bit her lip. "Do you remember his name? Was it Cole?" *Did she dare to hope she'd been the woman he had been referring to?*

"No, I don't think so, but then again, maybe. Wow, my head hurts." Frank's eyes closed, and his head drooped against his chest.

She'd have to be satisfied with that answer. Frank looked ready to pass out. If he did, there was no way she could carry him inside. "Let's get you inside." She helped Frank to his feet and ushered him inside the building and into his apartment, where he promised to call her if he needed anything or happened to remember the name of her visitor.

Inside her apartment, Madison dialed her parent's number in California. She hoped they wouldn't be too disappointed by her sudden change of plans, especially since she'd only accepted their invitation a few days before.

Her mother answered after the third ring, sounding out of breath. "Madison? Where are you? Your father and I were just leaving to go pick you up at the airport. Is something wrong?"

"No, everything's fine. Unfortunately, I have to change my plans again. I won't be able to come for Christmas because..." Excitement crept into her voice.

"You've met a man, haven't you?" Her mother interrupted. "I knew it." She sounded thrilled.

Madison hesitated and sighed. *What could she say?* She *had* in fact met a man, a wonderful man, but she didn't think it was a story to tell her mother right now. Things hadn't worked out between her and Cole. Right now she just wanted to share good news.

"No, mom, that's not it. It's my book. It has been accepted for publication, and I need to work on it over the holidays." A wide smile spread across her face as she pulled out a chair to sit. She kicked off her boots.

"Oh, honey, that's so wonderful. I'm so proud of you. When will I be able to read the final copy?" The sound of a car horn honking outside on her mother's end of the line startled her. "Oops, your father is still waiting for me in the car. I'd better go tell him the change of plans and of course, your wonderful news…" Her mother hesitated. "and you're sure there's no man?" She sounded disappointed.

"No, mom, unfortunately not."

* * * *

Madison sealed the sandwich bag containing the remaining twenty-seven chocolate oatmeal cookies and placed them in the pantry. She yawned and stretched. A glance at the clock on the microwave revealed it was almost midnight. Happy with the day's progress of three chapters revised and eight cookies eaten, she turned off the lights and headed to her bedroom.

She turned on her bedside lamp and pulled back the flannel sheets on the bed. Her cell phone blinked with unheard voice messages, but she ignored them. She'd heard the phone ring numerous times throughout the evening, but the ring tone had been Damien's. She refused to deal with him just yet. She'd emailed him an official letter of resignation that afternoon.

She crawled between the warm, soft sheets, and her cell phone beeped with a new text message. She hesitated, wondering who would be texting her this late at night. If it was an emergency, Sam would call. She picked up the phone and checked the message I.D. *Cole? What did he want this late?*

Where are you? The message read.

At home. Alone, two days before Christmas, bursting at the seams to tell you my good news, she didn't add.

Guess where I am.

Seriously? It was after midnight. She wasn't in the mood for guessing games with him. *In a hot tub with a beautiful Australian girl.* Annoyed, she flung back the bed sheets and paced the floor in her bedroom.

In California with you parents.

Madison's mouth gaped, and she reread each word over again. *Were her sleepy eyes fooling her? What was he doing there?*

She dialed his cell number. This wasn't something that could be discussed through text messages. She sat on the edge of her bed biting her thumbnail as the phone rang. She stood and paced again. *Come on, answer.*

"Madison, hi." His sleepy, emotion-filled voice was the best thing she'd heard in two days.

"What are you doing in California?" She couldn't believe how absurd this season was becoming. She was no longer sure whether to laugh or cry at any given moment.

"I love you." Cole's voice was raw with emotion.

Tears stung Madison's eyes. "What about the girl in your studio today?" She paused near her bedroom window, looking out at the falling snow.

"I love you," Cole repeated.

"But you were so angry at the law Christmas party—and I haven't heard from you..." Her rambling made no sense, even to her own ears.

"Madison, I love you." He repeated for the third time.

Who cares about anything else? Not her, not at that moment. He loved her. "I love you too Cole," she whispered. Her heart felt about to explode with happiness.

"Explain to me how I am spending Christmas in a snowless, treeless place, with your parents and *you* are still in New York?" His tone pleaded.

She laughed through the tears streaming down her cheeks. "I didn't go. I had to work on my book."

"Your book? You mean your article?" Cole sounded confused.

"No, I mean my book. My manuscript was accepted!" Finally she was able to share this with him.

"Oh Madison, I am so proud of you. I wish I could hold you and kiss your head, your cheeks, your lips and your beautiful, perfect little nose."

"Come back." She couldn't wait to see him again.

"I'm booked on the next flight out." Cole sounded eager to be back in New York.

She was eager to have him back. "I'll be waiting at the airport."

Chapter Eleven

Cole's flight landed at ten-thirty the next morning, and Madison was at the airport at ten o'clock, in case the flight arrived early. The airport was full of people arriving and leaving for their holiday destinations, and she found herself caught up in the excitement of it all. Everyone had somewhere special to be, or someone special to share the season with, and this year, so did she. She yawned as she paced in front of the arrivals gate. She hadn't slept the night before as they'd spent hours text messaging each other.

Cole explained that he'd been developing photos in his dark room when she'd come to see him. His young visitor had been *Miss Teen Manhattan* getting her publicity shots done earlier that day at his studio. Madison couldn't believe she'd been jealous of a young, teenage girl with an attitude, but how was she to know? He said the moment the young girl had given him the message, he'd walked out of his meeting with the *Gucci* executives and had gone in search of her. He'd tried her apartment, then the office.

Samantha had been the one to inform him Madison had quit her job and was headed to California for Christmas. He hadn't even packed any clothes and boarded the next flight to California to find her. Arriving at her family home, he'd discovered she wasn't there, but her parents had been kind enough to let him stay. He had apologized for leaving her with Kurt and how miserable he'd been for the last few days—thinking things were over between them. Sending the photos had been his next to last attempt at getting her back. The last attempt was submitting one awful manuscript to her after another, he had teased.

At first, Madison didn't see him, as the passengers came filling through the busy terminal, then a miniature, decorated Christmas tree poked its way through the crowd. She smiled at the sight as Cole came toward her.

He dropped the tree to the floor and wrapped his arms around her. "Madison, it feels like forever since I've seen you," he whispered into her hair.

She wrapped her arms tight around his neck. Even in his rumpled clothing and tousled hair, he looked amazing. "I can't believe you flew to California."

Cole kissed her forehead, her cheeks, her neck not caring about the crowds of people around them, watching their open display of affection. "Let's get out of here. I could use a shower."

"Um, that sounds like a great idea." Madison's eyes glinted as they met his.

Cole stopped and turned her to face him, intrigue and desire written all over his face. "Madison, you better promise not to fight with me this time." He warned, "I don't think I could handle that again. I had to walk halfway around Tuscumbia to cool off the last time."

* * * *

Two days later, Madison awoke to the smell of pancakes, bacon and eggs cooking in her apartment. Entering the kitchen, she smiled. Cole cooked breakfast while hanging white Christmas lights in her kitchen window.

"What are you doing?' Madison yawned and stretched. She leaned against the counter, smiling.

"Oh good, you're up. What do you think? Do you want an evergreen tree or a blue spruce?" Cole struggled with the lights in one hand, spatula in the other.

"I think I want a *good morning* and a kiss."

Cole grinned as he dropped the spatula onto the stove. "Good morning, little lady." He picked her up and set her on top of the counter. He kissed her lips and brushed a strand of dark hair from her shoulder. "Now, evergreen or blue spruce?"

"What's wrong with the tree we have? I've grown attached to it." Madison left a trail of tiny kisses along his neck and down his bare chest. She could get used to having him cook breakfast for her like this. The day before had been nothing short of amazing, as they hadn't left her apartment. They'd taken their shower as promised and spent hours wrapped in each others arms on Madison's living room sofa. They hadn't needed to talk, they were content to be next to each other at last, feeling the warmth and love radiating between them. For dinner, they'd ordered a pizza, and Cole had insisted on reading her manuscript. Sharing it with him had been wonderful.

"It's great, but if we are having Christmas in this apartment tomorrow, we need to make this place a little more festive." His words faltered as her mouth reached his belly.

"Madison, it's hard to focus with you doing that."

"Okay. I choose an evergreen." Madison jumped from the counter and headed for the kitchen door.

"Hey, where are you going? I was enjoying that."

Madison laughed. "To shower and dress. We have a lot of work to do if we want to make this place look festive." She didn't own a single Christmas decoration, and she agreed with Cole, this Christmas should be special. They had invited Samantha and her family to Christmas dinner and had also extended the invitation to the Thompson family, who had accepted. Scott was happy not to have to cook a turkey, and the girls were excited to see Madison again.

Coming out of the shower a few minutes later, her mail sat on the counter. "So, I guess you met Frank in your search for me the other day?" She towel dried her hair.

"If you mean the short, balding man who riddled me with questions, then yes." Cole laughed. "He seemed jealous. Do you two have something going on?"

Madison shrugged. "You never know. He is cute." She picked up her mail. On top of the pile was her copy of *Women's World Quarterly* magazine. She tossed it aside and flipped through the rest of her mail.

"Aren't you going to look at that?" Cole gestured toward the magazine. He climbed down from the stepladder and plugged in the Christmas lights.

"No, the wound hasn't healed yet." She'd gotten over the fact she no longer worked for the publication, but she wasn't ready to read an article written to replace her own.

"But, isn't that the original cover design?" Cole picked up the magazine.

Madison glanced at the cover. Her name and the bachelor article were toward the top of the page. *How had that happened?* They must have made a mistake at the press. She flipped to the second section of the magazine. There it was. "They published it." Madison wore a look of shock. Damien liked it after all.

"So they published it with only four bachelors?" Cole studied the article over her shoulder.

"Um, no. I used a replacement bachelor." Madison hid the magazine behind her back. Her face flushed. She hadn't yet told him she'd written about him as bachelor number five. She hadn't expected it to end up in print.

"Madison, who'd you write about?" Cole's eyes narrowed. His tone suggested he already knew the answer.

"No one you know." Madison dashed from the kitchen, but he was too quick for her.

"Let me see." He grabbed her and tickled her ribs.

"No." She squealed as he tickled her to the couch and stole the magazine.

"You wrote about me?" His face wore a look of disbelief, as he skimmed the article.

Madison didn't answer. She hid behind a cushion and waited for his reaction.

Cole flipped to the beginning of the article.

New York holds a reputation as one of the most exciting cities in America, filled with important, successful and interesting people, such as the five men featured in this article. For the last three weeks, I have been fortunate enough to meet with five of New York's most eligible bachelors and spend three wonderful, fun filled, adventurous days with each, observing their holiday traditions. A whirlwind tour from Manhattan to Whistler, to Tuscumbia and back again, there was never a dull moment along the way.

Bachelor number one, Scott Thompson, a successful real estate broker in Manhattan. A single father to two beautiful little girls, Amelia and Emma, this dad is a hardworking entrepreneur and role model to his daughters. Spending three days in the Thompson's beautiful Manhattan home was a spirit reviving respite, as the girls and their father invited me to participate in their family's holiday traditions. Snowball fights, Christmas tree hunting, and cookie baking were only the beginning for this active trio. An endearing and thoughtful visit to the children's hospital with toys for the sick children, one of their yearly traditions, was the highlight of my time with them. While Scott is one of New York's most successful, handsome men, it is his compassionate and kind soul that truly makes him a unique and special bachelor.

The next bachelor on my list was overnight sensation Gucci designer, Nathan Harper. However, bad news ladies, this one will not be a bachelor for long. The rumours are true, I was with him as Nathan scoured the Manhattan Tiffany store, braving the Christmas crowds for a perfect two carat diamond solitaire ring he recently placed upon girlfriend and model Becca Sambura's finger. Work never takes a break in the world of high fashion and Nathan's holidays were filled with fashion show rehearsals and photo shoots, presenting his new spring designs, which I will tell you first hand are incredible, as usual. This Texas born hottie is also a family man in the making as he spent time with fiancé Becca's family, even turning down tickets to a 'Giants' football game. A rare catch indeed. Hold onto him Becca.

Then I hopped a plane to Whistler, British Columbia where Blake Ford, Bachelor number three was spending the season in the climate and surroundings he loves best—his winter home on the slopes. This Olympic snowboarding gold medalist is a well-known face in the Whistler Village. Locals and tourists alike enjoy free snowboard and ski lessons from the handsome, young, former U.S. Marine. By the way ladies, he still keeps that 'Marine' body. Raised by his grandparents, with a humble beginning to life, Blake Ford is a thoughtful, adventure seeking man with a smile that warms the entire mountain. He is single and claims to be looking for that special someone who can keep him on his toes. Lace up those snow boots ladies and hit the slopes for a chance at this man's heart.

Bachelor number four may live in downtown Manhattan where his successful medical practice takes up five floors of the Trump Tower Building, but Rod Livingston's heart can be found in Tuscumbia, Alabama during the holiday season. Having spent three days in the wonderful Christmas oriented town, I can understand why. The entire community comes together at that time of year and everything revolves around the season. The town's re-enactment of 'A Christmas Carol' is the highlight of the festivities, and their outdoor skating rink is a hotspot for local romance. When asked if there was romance in the air for Rod himself this season, the shy bachelor refuses to comment, but the mischievous gleam in his eye tells a different story. Spending time with the Livingston family in Tuscumbia was truly a remarkable experience. Who could resist falling in love with a man who dresses as a reindeer each holiday season to put a smile on the faces of local children?

Bachelor number five was someone I was fortunate enough to spend the entire season with, as he traveled with me, photographing each of these handsome men. Award winning photographer, Cole Harris is New York's best kept secret in the world of photography, with his talent outweighed only by his compassionate and caring nature. While we got off to a rocky start to the assignment, it wasn't long before Cole's easygoing nature and passion for life and his work melted my thick resolve, and this bachelor soon had a place for himself in my heart as a true friend. His work alone is worthy of this man's place as bachelor number five in this year's review of New York's finest men. However, when you combine his mischievous grin and fervent determination, this man captures our attention and our hearts. His volunteer work with local children's charities and being the favorite uncle to his beautiful nieces, places this bachelor as number one on my list of people I'd love to spend any and every holiday with.

As the season draws near, my heart is filled with love and joy as I watch the hope and happiness spread all around, from Manhattan to Whistler to Tuscumbia, and everywhere else. Through my travels this holiday season, I've learned it doesn't matter where you are in the world, the spirit of Christmas will always find you there.

"Wow, is that how you see me?" Cole finished reading the article and closed the magazine.

"I meant every word." Madison let the pillow fall back to the couch.

Cole kissed the palm of her hand, his eyes never leaving hers. "Then how about spending every holiday with me?"

"Are you asking me to be your girlfriend?" Madison smiled.

"I'm asking you to marry me." Cole's tone was serious, quiet—his feelings for her written all over his handsome face.

Madison's eyes welled with tears of happiness, and she flung her arms around him.

"Is that a *yes*?" Cole laughed and squeezed her tight.

Madison leaned back and brought her lips to his. "Yes, bachelor number five, yes."

The End

About the Author

Jennifer Snow lives in Edmonton, Alberta with her fiancé and two year old son. Writing contemporary romance fiction, her previous works include Mistletoe Fever and Mistletoe & Molly. A member of the RWA and the Alberta Writer's Guild, she is active in the writing community with author pages on Shewrites.com, Backspace.org, and Goodreads.com. For information on upcoming releases, please visit her website at www.jennifersnowbooks.com

Secret Cravings Publishing
www.secretcravingspublishing.com